THE Webbed Hand

Ferrian smiled at her, showing those sharp, yellowing teeth. "Now you're here in Rienzi Maria, now that we're so soon to be united as one, it hardly matters your knowing. You have to realize that Fireflies are used to guard this castle. There is no escape from here. So I can afford to tell you that there is a defence.

"Water. They cannot stand water. It is not entirely a drawback. It means that we can control them, borrowing the arts of aquemancy. We can transport them from one end of Maquerlia to the other, in specially constructed cages." He paused, tilting Maria's face up towards his own. "We could get them to Soprafini itself in a matter of weeks, my dear," he said to her. "I expect your father would be most interested to see the Fireflies feed, don't you agree? We must arrange it, one day."

Maria said nothing. But Philippa had never seen her look so white.

Also in the Point Fantasy series:

THE Webbed Hand

Jenny Jones

Scholastic Children's Books,
Scholastic Publications Ltd,
7–9 Pratt Street, London NW1 OAE, UK

Scholastic Inc.,
555 Broadway, New York, NY 10012, USA

Scholastic Canada Ltd,
123 Newkirk Road, Richmond Hill,
Ontario, Canada L4C 3G5

Ashton Scholastic Pty Ltd,
P O Box 579, Gosford, New South Wales,
Australia

Ashton Scholastic Ltd,
Private Bag 92801, Penrose, Auckland,
New Zealand

First published by Scholastic Publications Ltd, 1994

Text copyright © Jenny Jones, 1994
Cover illustration copyright © David Scutt, 1994

ISBN 0 590 55649 5

Typeset by TW Typesetting, Midsomer Norton, Avon
Printed by Cox & Wyman Ltd, Reading, Berks

For Henry, with love

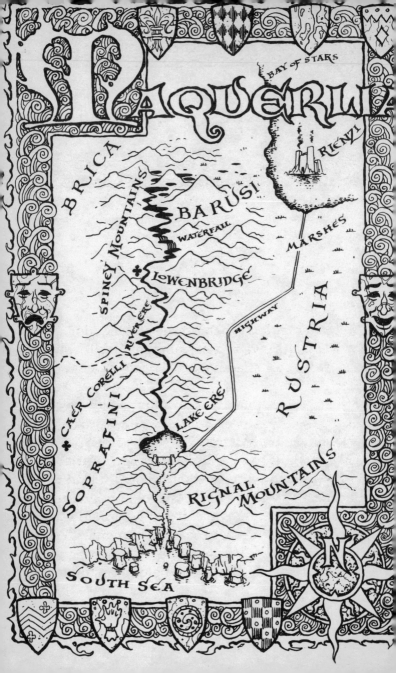

The doors closed behind the ambassador. Maria turned to her mother. "Well!" she said, her eyes sparkling. "At last! Queen of Rustria!"

"It is a great honour," said Olivia. Her voice was as colourless as ever. "You will have to conduct yourself with dignity."

"Much is invested in this marriage, Maria. I hardly need to tell you what this will mean to our country." Maria's father, Gregor of Soprafini, did not bother to look at his daughter. He was still scanning the betrothal agreement. "We shall be relying on you not to let us down."

Maria wasn't listening. She held her hand up

to the light, regarding the glittering outsize stone on her fourth finger. "Diamond mines," she said softly. "They have diamond mines and gold in the mountains and pearls in the oyster beds of Rustria. The Crown Jewels will be magnificent."

"Of course they will be," said Gregor sharply. "It is an enormously wealthy, powerful country. You are more fortunate than you know, Maria. You will have the best of everything."

"The best of everything!" repeated Maria to her maid Philippa that night. She was getting ready for bed, after a day of high excitement. "Of course, I will take my own trousseau, although I'm sure Rustrian fashions will be the height of elegance—"

"Their ambassador was bald," observed Philippa.

"Don't be ridiculous. It was just cut very short."

Philippa wondered whether the Rustrian women had to shave their hair too, but it was hardly the kind of question the Princess Maria would welcome.

"I think you're going to have to sharpen up your manners and attitudes before we go to Rustria," Maria continued. "Everything will be very different there, and I don't want you letting me down. In fact, it may be best to leave you behind."

Philippa continued to fold clothes, unmoved. She doubted whether this was a serious threat. She was too valuable to Maria to be left behind. Who else would put up with the tantrums and bad temper?

A diversion was required. "What about the Lord Lassan, my lady?" she asked.

Maria stood up and went to the window. Her long blonde hair flowed down her back. "It's going to be hard," she sighed. "I'll never forget my first love—"

As if on cue, a reedy tenor voice drifted through the open window. He'd been waiting for her to appear, Philippa reckoned. You could always rely on Lassan Legrenzi to get the timing right.

"*My heart will weep forever,*" he sang, plucking away at a lute.

"There he is!" Maria gazed dreamily down at her beloved. "Oh, Lassan!" she whispered, leaning forward over the window sill.

He stood on the grass below the window, his pale hair shining in the moonlight. He was positioned so that Maria might enjoy an uninterrupted view of his excellent profile. Perfect white teeth gleamed at her. "*Princess of delight, queen of my dreams,*" he sang, and then took a step nearer. "Maria, is this true? You're really going to marry that northern barbarian?"

"Ferrian is not a barbarian!"

"You've never even met him. They're all barbarians in Rustria, everyone knows that. Oh, Maria, how could you throw away our love like this?"

"It is my destiny. I have to marry Ferrian to save Soprafini." This was melodramatic, but true. Rustria was expanding its empire and Soprafini was next in line. Maria's marriage to the Prince of Rustria had been planned from the moment of her birth, in the hopes that the mighty Rustrians would leave Soprafini alone. So far it had worked.

The marriage would seal the alliance.

Still. "Oh Lassan, I'll never forget you," said Maria, her hands clasped at her throat.

"I'll come for you, Maria!" He sounded so passionate. "Just send me a word and I'll be there. If they really are as awful as everyone says you don't have to stay—"

She gazed at him, enchanted. This was real devotion. He was so truly handsome, so faithful and loyal. She plucked a rose from the bowl on the window sill and threw it down to him.

Tears filled her eyes as she watched him catch it and press it to his lips.

So poignant, to leave true love behind.

But Maria of Soprafini was going to be Queen of Rustria and could not be diverted by affairs of the heart, no matter how passionate.

She had no real regrets, not one.

Later that summer the Soprafinian wedding party left Caer Corelli to travel to Rustria. Prince Ferrian was sending a military escort to take over from the Soprafinians at Lake Ere, on the border of the two countries.

Gregor and Olivia's presence was not required at the wedding. Ferrian had made this very clear, but Maria was disappointed. It was not that they were a particularly affectionate family; nothing could be further from the truth. The Soprafinian Royal Family preserved a cool and formal attitude to one another at all times. Maria had, however, wanted to impress her parents.

She had spent all her sixteen years trying to find some way of pleasing them but nothing had worked. This at least would move them, Maria thought, the marriage of their only offspring to the most powerful man in five continents. It was a cloud on Maria's gilded horizon that they were not going to be present at her triumph, but she shed more tears over Lassan.

Philippa shed tears over no one. Servants weren't expected to have feelings.

*   *   *

The journey went smoothly, although the Soprafinian roads were full of pot-holes. They arrived at the lake later than arranged because a tree had blocked the road at one point. It was almost midnight. Halfway across the road that ran along the top of the dam, Maria and Philippa could see the Rustrian carriage waiting for them, outlined by flickering torchlight.

They were helped out of the Soprafinian state carriage and into the Rustrian by a tall Captain of the Soprafinian guard. There was no moon and in the dark they could see nothing of their surroundings. The Captain took Maria's arm to guide her to the Rustrian carriage, but Philippa had to find her own way.

For a moment she delayed, her hands on the rail at the top of the dam. She could hear the rushing of the water through the sluice gates far below and shivered. A sudden gust of cold air lifted through her hair, a sharp reminder that winter was coming. It felt very lonely and wild. And then Maria called to her and she hurried to her mistress's side.

The Captain stood to attention in the torch-light, saluting as the Rustrian carriage drew away, and only Philippa looked back.

This was her last glance of Soprafini, lost in the windy black depths of night. It was the only home she'd ever known, although she'd never been happy there. That hadn't mattered, servants didn't expect happiness. But she had felt inexplicably uneasy and nervous, crossing that dam into Rustria. Better the devil you know, she thought, worriedly. She glanced at Maria, wondering if she was feeling the same.

Maria was suffering no such qualms. She was exclaiming over the streamlined design of the Rustrian coach, delighting in the velvet upholstery, the fur rugs and lavish refreshments laid out for them. There were meat pasties and flagons of dark red wine, and heavy cakes made of treacle and clotted cream.

"Don't they have vegetables in Rustria?" asked Philippa in dismay. "Don't they grow fruit?"

"For heaven's sake, Philippa! I really hope you're not going to display such ignorance once we get to Rienzi! These pasties are made from venison! This is Brican claret!"

However, Philippa noticed that Maria actually ate very little. She had always been finicky about food. If this stodgy stuff was typical of Rustrian cuisine, Maria was in for a hard time.

They were speeding along a wide highway, leading down from the Spiney Mountains to the coastal plains of Rustria. No pot-holes or ruts here, no fallen trees or difficult gradients. Philippa had the impression that everything run by the Rustrians went smoothly.

Their carriage was beautifully sprung. Their outriders, grim-faced men with pistols and swords, were courteous enough. They were travelling at great speed.

Maria chattered away to Philippa, exclaiming at every sight, every town and landscape, as if it was the most delightful thing she'd ever seen.

Delightful? Philippa thought differently. Most of Rustria seemed flat and uninteresting to her. There were miles and miles of low, damp fields divided by stagnant ditches. Some areas were flooded and the grey waters reflected the cloudy sky. The only trees they saw were stubby, pollarded willows. There were no forests or woods anywhere.

The towns were drab, built on a grid system, crammed with stone built houses with flat roofs. There were very few people to be seen. Philippa wondered if people had been told to stay indoors when the coach passed. Sometimes they came across a scattering of peasants working in the fields but no one looked up as they passed.

Every now and then they saw in the distance a training camp, groups of buildings squatting round a parade ground where men in gaudy uniforms marched in squares.

After ten days on the road, even Maria's spirits were beginning to fail. The drab countryside was enough to depress anyone. "When will we be there?" she asked one of the outriders at last.

"Tomorrow, my lady," said the man, his face stony. Philippa watched him curiously. She had never seen any of these men smile, not even when they stopped in the evenings at various inns on the way. These halts had clearly been planned with precision by the Rustrians. The girls were always ushered into private rooms and served there by one or more of the outriders. They had no opportunity of meeting the ordinary people.

Their guard never relaxed, never put away their knives and pistols, even when serving at the table. Their shaven heads made them look rather brutal, for all their courteous manner. From the way their clothes hung, Philippa rather thought that they wore body armour.

Philippa was puzzled. Rustria was not at war, not just at that moment. And yet the guardsmen sent by Prince Ferrian were armed as if for battle. Perhaps the country was overrun with highwaymen and brigands, thought Philippa, but they encountered no obstacles or delays.

"Rustria is such an orderly country," said Maria in approval. "They've got things beautifully under control."

"Perhaps they just like wearing weapons all

the time. Perhaps it's all the latest thing, fashionable . . ." offered Philippa, thoughtfully. But it didn't seem very likely.

Next day they crossed the last part of the interminable coastal plain and reached Rienzi, Prince Ferrian's island castle in the Bay of Stars.

It stood in the centre of the bay, a great heap of solid grey masonry. Blank, windowless walls rose high and sheer above the water. A solitary flag in blue and silver fluttered from one of the towers.

Maria and Philippa were carried from the mainland on an elaborately decorated ferry, hung with cloth of silver, carpeted in blue velvet. The ferry entered the castle through an arch overhung by a portcullis.

Uniformed guardsmen lined the quay, and the sound of trumpets echoed around the enclosing walls.

Prince Ferrian came forward to take Maria's hand as she stepped down the gangplank.

He was a slight figure, dressed in military fashion. Rows of medals on jewelled ribbons lined his thin chest.

"Welcome to Rienzi, Princess Maria," he said formally. "Welcome to your new home."

His hair was shorn, and his eyes were bulbous. Thin lips curled over sharply pointed teeth.

Philippa thought she had never seen a more cruel face.

Two weeks later, on the eve of the wedding, all Philippa's worst fears were realized.

There had been endless ceremonies, interminable banquets and speeches and receptions. Every spare moment was taken up with lectures on the history and customs of Rustria. The result of all this activity was that Maria spent very little time with Ferrian. He bowed to her across the crowded halls, and sat next to her at entertainments, although they hardly talked. It was probably just as well, Philippa thought. She didn't think that Ferrian was going to improve on acquaintance.

For light relaxation the two girls were conducted all over the Castle by Tracho, Ferrian's personal assistant. Ferrian had apparently given instructions that Maria should be shown her new home, although he couldn't be bothered to do the job himself.

Tracho was an elderly man, always dressed in heavy brocade robes. He was elaborately courteous, if somewhat distant. Pompous, Philippa decided. But she didn't dare say so to Maria, who would hear no criticism of anything or anyone in Rustria. The Princess of Soprafini was determined to make a success of her marriage.

Tracho showed them the stables and the armouries and the chambers where strange weapons were being assembled. "Part of our defensive capabilities," he said coolly. "And in the workshops along here, we are developing machines which can send these weapons further than the eye can see." He lifted a hand and Maria and Philippa were treated to a short demonstration.

Maria was impressed. "But who on earth would ever attack Rustria?" she said. "No one would dare!"

Tracho smiled at her. There was more than a trace of mockery in his expression. "We are fortunate to find such wisdom in our new Princess," he said. "But there are occasional rebellions, and some of our neighbours do not quite understand the advantages of Rustrian civilization. Now do follow me . . ." They set off through a set of double doors. It was only a little later that Maria inadvertently took a wrong turning, starting off down an unmarked, brightly lit corridor.

"Not down there!" He clawed at her shoulder, pulling her back. "I'm sorry, my lady. There's nothing to interest you there," he said, more calmly. "If you are not too tired, lady, allow me to show you what we call the brewery. . . ."

They traipsed through a great gallery filled with foul smells and bubbling barrels of disgusting liquid. There were strangely masked people tending these barrels, stirring, pouring and mixing. Great swathes of noxious gas billowed around them.

By the end of this particular tour, both Maria and Philippa felt more than a little sick.

That evening, as they were getting ready for dinner, Maria realized that she had dropped one of her earrings on that afternoon's tour.

"Go and find it for me, will you?" she ordered Philippa. "It must have happened when that ridiculous man grabbed me this afternoon." And then she paused. A sharp look came over her otherwise pretty features. "Just a minute. I'll come too. Let's go and see whatever it was Tracho wouldn't show us. I don't see why things should be hidden from me here."

Philippa took a deep breath. "Will we have time, my lady?" She didn't like questioning Maria's decisions.

Maria shrugged. "Of course. I can remember the way, can't you? But if anyone tries to stop us, we'll just say that we're lost, looking for the earring."

It felt dangerous, walking through those long corridors without escort. No one challenged them. Uniformed men merely bowed, and opened doors for them.

Maria knew where they were going. She'd made it her business to know all she could about her future home. Unerringly, she led Philippa down several staircases. They were in luck. Almost as soon as they reached the stairwell on the fifth level, they smelled the stink of the poison vats. "Down there," said Maria confidently. "And to the right."

The brightly-lit corridor wound out of sight, and on the floor at their feet lay Maria's golden earring.

Philippa picked it up. She said hesitantly, "Lady, let's go back now. We don't want to offend—"

"Philippa, tomorrow I'm going to be married

to Ferrian. Everything in this castle will be mine. It's ridiculous to think of them hiding things from me!"

She flounced off down the corridor and Philippa trailed miserably behind.

There was no one there. No soldiers lining the walls or guarding the doors. Maria's step slowed. For all their bravado, they were beginning to creep along like guilty children. And then they came to the first of the cages.

It was set in the wall, a thick wire mesh nearly masking its contents. A pair of orange eyes stared at them from the gloom. "It's a ronal lion!" said Maria, in wonder. These were big cats, almost extinct in Soprafini, remarkable for their black and white speckled fur.

It lay there against the straw, listlessly regarding them. Maria moved on, and the corridor opened up into a large gallery, full of cages and aquaria and aviaries. Animals growled and birds screamed. There were insects and fishes, creatures that they knew well and others they had never seen before.

This was a menagerie, full of unusual and obscure animals. "Why ever wouldn't they show us *this*?" cried Maria, enchanted by a vast, brilliant blue-coloured butterfly. It had a wingspan of over a metre. In another cage, a monkey with four arms was cradling its offspring. There were blue lizards and gerrypuns, branticores and remickles . . .

"What are you doing here?"

Philippa gasped and spun round. At her side, she was aware that Maria had gone white.

An armoured monster stood before them. Someone clad in bizarrely constructed yellow armour, helmeted and visored.

A hand shielded with spikes and studs pushed back the visor and Ferrian's unpleasant face came into view.

It *would* be Ferrian. Philippa nervously clutched her hands together.

"My lord," said Maria, her voice only a little higher than usual. "I lost my earring in our tour this morning. We merely came to fetch it—"

"What have you got servants for? And don't tell me that Tracho brought you here, for I know he did not."

His voice was cold.

"I thought you wished me to acquaint myself with Rustrian ways, with the castle here—"

"Don't be more stupid than you can help." There was a silence while he looked at them.

They heard the sound of feet from somewhere beyond Ferrian. Several soldiers marched up to him and one of them saluted.

"Well?" Ferrian said, turning his attention to them.

"The Fireflies are ready, sire," the soldier replied.

Fireflies? Philippa looked at the man in puzzlement.

He didn't seem to be joking. Hardly anyone in Rustria ever joked. But she didn't believe in the existence of Fireflies. Stories to frighten children, she'd always thought. On a level with ogres and unicorns and mermaids. They'd seen strange animals here, but nothing like that . . . She wondered what the Rustrians were up to.

"Well, well." Ferrian seemed to have made up his mind. "Well, ladies, seeing as you are here, and so curious, perhaps I may be permitted to show you something of our more – unusual – Rustrian skills." He made a sign to the soldiers, and beckoned for the two girls to follow.

They crossed the gallery and went through a pair of vast double doors into another huge room. There was a railing running round an area in its centre. A man brought them protective clothing – not full scale armour like Ferrian's, but heavy plated visors and gauntlets – and helped them put them on. He stood rigidly to attention as Ferrian motioned them forward.

"Now," he said, leading them to the railing. They were standing looking over a widely yawning pit, set deep into the ground. It was quite empty. "You'll have a good view from here. I've arranged for the Fireflies to be fed, you see. I'm sure you'll find it interesting."

"Sir, I did not know that the Fireflies lived outside stories." Maria was recovering slightly.

"The flying dragons of the ancient days do not exist," Ferrian had replied, with some smugness. "No, these are something different; something much more interesting. They are my own creation. I have studied with the masters, I have sacrificed much in the pursuit of knowledge." He leaned towards Maria, and Philippa saw her blink. Bad breath, she thought, unsurprised. Of course he'd have bad breath. "There is a way to balance the elements, you see. There are people who concentrate on water-magic, or on stone-shifting. You may have heard of such people."

His pale eyes flickered over to Philippa and she wondered if he mistrusted her. She comforted herself with the thought that it would be just like Ferrian to make other people feel uncomfortable.

He was still talking. "I have used alchemical principles to weld together two of the elements, wind and air. Some call this process pyromancy, but I prefer to think of it as scientific. It is a dangerous, highly skilled process. In so doing, I have found a way to strike at the heart of life itself.

"The superstitious talk of pacts with God. I have made a different kind of bargain." He smiled. "But do not be afraid, my Maria. I have devoted my life to creation, not destruction. I have created beings of fire and air, which I honour with the name 'Firefly'. I am delighted to be able to show you, my affianced bride, the fruits of my labours."

He raised his hand as a signal and a door to the side of the pit clanged open. The two girls leaned forward over the railing to catch their first sight of Ferrian's creatures.

They looked down, and a dragon screamed at them. There was a dazzling whirl of action below them. It was like looking into a living furnace. It was devastating, shocking. Neither of the girls had expected the Fireflies to move like that. It was impossible to see any details at all because they shifted from place to place in the space of a blink, flickering in a blaze of sulphurous smoke, blazing and roaring with impatience.

Heat battered on their visors and armour. But still, Philippa felt impelled to lean closer. The Fireflies were fascinating. She found herself trying to follow one of them, trying to make out a head, a limb, anything to reassure herself that this was indeed a living creature and not some terrible evil spirit, as Ferrian's words had implied. But however hard she concentrated, she could see nothing clearly. There was something repulsive about that agile movement, something deeply unsettling about their indistinct appearance.

The noise didn't help. High-pitched screams echoed and reverberated all around them.

"They can be heard on the mainland, if there's no wind," said Ferrian. He had flipped his visor aside and was watching Maria carefully, his hand like a fat slug on her elbow. Philippa saw his lips smile, but those blank fishy eyes were quite serious. They always were.

"We're just in time," he said gently. "I'd like you to watch this carefully. It's rather interesting." He nudged Maria forward, right to the edge of the pit.

A door clanged below them, and a young calf, bellowing pitifully, was pushed into the pit.

Maria tried to step back, but Ferrian wouldn't allow it. "This is the best place to get a really good view," he said, his hand moving to her shoulder. "Right here."

Philippa could not desert her mistress. So she stood there too and watched the Fireflies dance round the terrified calf, watch them tease it with little darts of flame, singeing its coat so that the smell of burnt hair overlaid the sulphur.

And then, in a rush too fast to see, they incinerated it.

A terrific blast of flame consumed the calf. Philippa could feel the violence of the heat crashing against her visor. The brilliance of the blaze forced her to shut her eyes.

When she opened them again the calf had vanished. There was nothing left of it at all, just a small pile of greying, drifting, ash.

The Fireflies sank back against the walls of the pit and for a moment Philippa saw them.

They were thin and bony, with long forearms and legs. Their heads were elongated, rather equine with long snouts, but their eyes were filled only with fire. At their shoulders, redundant wings hung like rags of smoke.

Then as they started to move again, to flicker in and out of her vision, she realized something horrible, something she could not quite get her mind round. "They've got no mouths!" she gasped, quite forgetting that servants didn't speak unless spoken to.

For once, the Princess Maria ignored the lapse. And Ferrian merely turned his unpleasant fishy stare towards her.

"That's right," he said, agreeably. "They don't *eat*, you see. Not what you or I would call eating. Watch now, this is important. . . ."

The clang of the gate once more. And three

terrified humans stumbled forward into the pit; two men and a woman. They were dressed in rags, probably captured during one of the Rustrians' "defensive" campaigns, Philippa thought. Two of them clung together, wailing miserably, but the other, a tall young man, fell on his knees clearly begging Ferrian for mercy. He spoke a language none of them could understand.

The Fireflies played no games with them.

As deaths go, it was quick. Another great blast of flame, the flaring light, the sick smell of charred flesh, the fall of dark ash . . .

Maria was pushing back from the edge of the pit, her fingers fumbling at the visor but Ferrian had hold of her arm. "Watch, my dear Maria," he said. "I *insist* you see this. View it as the start of the wedding celebrations." He smiled again, the thin lips drawn back.

And before their appalled gaze, they saw the darting action of the Fireflies become more intense, more vivid and extreme, filling the pit with flame and smoke and high-pitched, soaring song. . . .

And gradually, the two girls realized that there were no longer only three Fireflies in the pit. There were four of them now, flickering in and out of their vision, dancing some weird and horrible celebration.

"You see," said Ferrian to his betrothed, "the Fireflies are not animals at all. They have no mouths, as your slave has observed. They were created using the power of pyromancy, and were given life from the deaths of people who lost their lives in flame. Our preferred method of execution is death by fire, of course. Traitors, criminals, prisoners of war . . . There was a campaign some years ago to the north. We executed certain of our captives and made use of their deaths in this way."

His voice was totally cool and undisturbed. Maria had turned away from him, her hands to her mouth. Ferrian took no notice. "You see, my Fireflies absorb energy from their prey in the moment of its burning death. The priests put it a little differently. They say that the Fireflies seize the souls of those they incinerate. Souls, spirit, energy . . . Who knows?" He smiled. "All we know for sure is that animal prey does not satisfy them. All it does is calm them for a few moments. But the death of human prey causes them to reproduce.

"That's how I made them in the first place."

For a moment Philippa saw Maria sway slightly and wondered whether she was going to faint. But her mistress took a deep breath and remained silent while Philippa helped her out of the protective clothes.

"How many Fireflies are there?" Maria asked in a voice that was only a little unsteady.

"Over two hundred," said Ferrian, his large, watery eyes animated at last. "Their numbers are growing all the time, of course. And it is rather difficult to find the right quantity of – fuel – for them. You have many slaves in Soprafini, I hear."

"Not slaves," said Maria quickly. "Very few. There are many peasants working the land, but they are free—"

"Peasants, slaves, what's the difference?" Ferrian raised an eyebrow. "After tomorrow, they will be mine too."

"My father might have something to say about that," said Maria. "He is still king!"

"At the moment." Ferrian nodded. "Just remember, dear Maria, how powerful we Rustrians are now. I believe Tracho has shown you our armoury and workshops. And with over two hundred Fireflies as the heart of our army. . . ."

"Is there any defence against them?" Maria spoke desperately.

Ferrian smiled at her, showing those sharp, yellowing teeth. "Now you're here in Rienzi Maria, now that we're so soon to be united as one, it hardly matters your knowing. You have to realize that Fireflies are used to guard this castle. There is no escape from here. So I can afford to tell you that there is a defence.

"Water. They cannot stand water. It is not entirely a drawback. It means that we can control them, borrowing the arts of aquemancy. We can transport them from one end of Maquerlia to the other, in specially constructed cages." He paused, tilting Maria's face up towards his own. "We could get them to Soprafini itself in a matter of weeks, my dear," he said to her. "I expect your father would be most interested to see the Fireflies feed, don't you agree? We must arrange it, one day."

Maria said nothing. But Philippa had never seen her look so white.

CHAPTER 3

The wedding was the next day.

That evening, after the enormous banquet of rich and greasy food which constituted dinner, Philippa crept away.

She left Maria on her own, miserably writing her diary for the last time as Princess of Soprafini. Maria had been in a foul mood all evening. She had eventually dismissed Philippa and it was a relief.

Philippa had a secret. She had told no one, especially not Maria. Philippa had always been too scared to share it with her mistress. It was also illegal, both in Soprafini and Rustria.

She wound her cloak around her and ran

swiftly along the corridor outside Maria's private apartment. Soldiers stood on the other side of the double doors leading to the guest wing.

At the end of the corridor was a door which led to one of the servants' staircases. Philippa had found it some time ago, on one of her lone explorations while Maria underwent tuition.

The staircase led up to the roof. Philippa shut the door behind her and ran up the stairs, out on to the windy, rain-speckled rooftop.

It was deserted. There was no light, either from the moon or from the mainland. Somewhere in the castle below she heard a door clang, and someone shout.

She took a deep breath, bent down and scooped some rainwater from a gully. She held it in hands which were red with cold, and tried to settle her mind.

Impossible. This wasn't going to work. She was more scared than she had ever been before in her life. Her secret was going to desert her, just when she needed it.

Her hands were shaking, not only with cold, and the water was already trickling away. The wind was pulling at her long skirts, whipping them about her. It was difficult to see, difficult to make out the dance of light in the dark, reflective surface cupped in her hands.

Maria would be calling for her soon, she

always did. This was too great a risk. She should never have chanced it, it was useless, hopeless! She had snatched only a few brief minutes of privacy, but however hard she tried to clamp her hands together, every moment the water dripped through. . . .

It was starting to rain again, and for that at least she had to be grateful. The Fireflies wouldn't be out, not with rain around. But the raindrops were disturbing the surface of the water even further, and thoughts of the Fireflies did nothing to calm her mind. She crouched lower over her hands, praying to the unknown gods for a response. She had so little time, and discovery would be worse than death. What if it stopped raining and the Fireflies found her?

Please, went her thoughts. *We have no time, no time at all. Tomorrow will be too late, please show me what to do* . . . But still the wind screamed through her hair and clothes and she knew she was too frantic, too anxious for it to work and there was so little time. Only a few minutes, she told herself, it has to be now, it has to be now, while it's raining. They won't let the Fireflies out while it's raining . . . She kept trying to remember this, as if it were a magic charm, something to reassure in a situation where nothing else could help.

A deep breath to calm herself. Another, trying

to keep her thoughts quiet and empty. She looked at the water almost casually and all at once the mist cleared. This was her secret, her extraordinary, amazing, shameful skill.

She could see the truth in a pool of water.

She never called it magic, she never thought of it like that. It was just a tiny talent, a small diversion that usually led her into trouble. . . .

And yet she was always drawn to it, entrapped by the power of water.

The mists cleared and she saw between her hands a great lake, shimmering in moonlight. Her fingers were like mountains standing in silence round the lake, a soaring range of peaks just tipped with snow. The mountains were waiting for something. They were waiting for water to fall.

Was it rain they wanted? Water from the sky? There were no answers in this picture of heavy ominous hills, shadowy with forests, dark with the great turrets of stone and rock.

She turned her vision away from the mountains and concentrated on the lake. There was no wind, no disturbance to the surface, lightly shining in silver moonlight. But as she watched the shadow of a hand drifted over the water, a hand with webbing between the fingers. It passed over the water like a five-pointed cloud over the sun.

And then she saw that the waters were shifting. At one end they were beginning to fall away, to drop over some great chasm, crashing in foam and violence.

The waters were full of death. They left death behind them, they took death with them. There was a deadly blackness about that depth of water, shifting and moving under the shadow of a webbed hand.

The water was draining away from the centre of the lake, leaving it barren and empty, and for a moment she thought she was going to see what was revealed there.

Somewhere her mind registered footsteps, the regular marching of the guard's patrol.

She was breathing hard, her eyes glittering with the strain of staring so hard, so intently into the future. Beneath the lake, something beneath the lake. . . .

But the footsteps were coming closer and her hands trembled uncontrollably, and the last of the water escaped, falling, dripping, draining away. . . .

Philippa took off her wet cloak and bundled it down one of the laundry chutes in the upper corridor. In the distance, she could hear Maria's bell ringing impatiently. It wouldn't do to keep her waiting, not tonight.

Philippa set off down the corridor at a run, pausing only at the door to run cold, damp hands over her gown.

"Shall I do your hair now, my lady?" she asked, entering Maria's bedchamber.

"Where have you been, Philippa? Why did you leave me?"

There was that sharp edge to Maria's voice that Philippa recognized as fear. Like Philippa, Maria had been horrified by the visit to the Menagerie.

"I suppose you were off dreaming again . . . Ouch! Why are you always so clumsy, so careless?"

This was unjust. Philippa was never clumsy, never careless. Such tendencies had been beaten out of her years ago.

"I'm so sorry, my lady," she said meekly.

But Maria was right to be nervous, thought Philippa, as she brushed the long fine hair. Nervous, at the very least. In her shoes, Philippa would have been suicidal. Philippa could imagine no worse fate than to be married to Ferrian of Rustria.

And yet, what could Maria do? She was so alone at Castle Rienzi. No family, no friends. For the first time, Philippa began to question what had happened. They had all been so impressed by Ferrian's proposal that no one seemed to have noticed the extraordinary conditions attached to the marriage. Maria had been permitted to retain only the services of one servant, Philippa. There was no guard, no ambassador, no relation to see her through the two weeks before the marriage. The Rustrians had insisted on this, as a condition of the marriage, and no one had thought to query it.

It was not as if Maria and her servant were treated badly: their quarters, at the top of a tower at the north end of Rienzi, were comfortable enough, even if the furniture was heavy and ugly. Their food was adequate, although not at all to Maria's taste. Great plates of roast meat and stodgy puddings formed the centre of every meal. But there were fresh flowers most days, tight buds of blood-red roses. Clothes made of velvet and satin were brought to her rooms to be fitted. Strongly scented powders and perfumed oils were put ready for her bath.

Guards patrolled the battlements of the tower, men with shaven heads, heavily armed with strange, double-edged swords. They'd never seen the Fireflies before that day, but sometimes in the calm of the night Philippa had heard weird screaming, and shuddered. Now she knew what it was.

Every night they heard keys turning in the

locks at the end of the corridor. There were bars on all the larger windows.

Rienzi was an island fortress, a palace two miles distant from the mainland in the Sea of Stars and as far as Philippa knew, there was no way out.

There was no one to turn to.

The preparations had been completed. The Court dressmakers had done their bit, the coiffeuse, the manicurists. Maria had been bathed and pampered and swathed in silk and satin and treated much like a doll. There had been a full dress-rehearsal in the Chapel with one of the guards standing in for Ferrian.

Everything was set. And then they had seen the Fireflies.

Maria had gone through the evening as if in a dream. She had smiled and bowed and said not a word out of place. But Philippa, watching her, knew that a breakdown of some kind was not far away.

At bedtime, Philippa had managed to pacify Maria, by listening sympathetically, by bringing her warm milk and honey, by singing softly the songs of their shared childhood. They had always been together. Philippa was an orphan, given to Maria on the Princess's third birthday, and they had never been apart since then.

She knew Maria through and through,

although she never admitted it. She was Maria's servant, not her friend. Maria never forgot it.

That night, Philippa wondered briefly whether to share her secret knowledge with Maria. But water-power of any kind was hated and feared in Soprafini and Philippa herself mistrusted the whole thing. They had both been brought up to think of water magic as the province of swindlers and frauds.

It wouldn't help, even if her vision had offered a gleam of hope, of comfort, something that might soothe Maria, and help her get through the next day.

But the drowned valley seemed irrelevant, something incomprehensible, the webbed hand verging on the horrific. Philippa understood not one part of her vision. She could not possibly share it with Maria. There was no relief there.

The hair-brushing was completed. But instead of moving to the ornate four-poster bed, Maria sat perfectly still for a moment.

"Do you think that Lassan will forget me?" she said so quietly that Philippa almost missed it.

"Never," she said with certainty. She knew that Lassan Legrenzi, he of the reedy tenor voice and flowery turn of phrase, would boast to the end of his days that he had been loved by Maria Soprafini before she became Queen of Rustria. And although Philippa hadn't liked Lassan, although she thought him vain and shallow, she could hardly blame her mistress for remembering Lassan with longing.

Her love for Lassan was a childhood dream and would have to be forgotten. It was all in the past.

"Philippa, what am I going to do?" A crack in Maria's voice, a most unusual loss of control.

"My lady, you will look beautiful, you will be honoured through Maquerlia, and Prince Ferrian—"

"But I hate him!" she cried. "He makes my skin crawl. I can't bear to be near him, he revolts me! And then those Fireflies! Those monsters! What if he attacks Soprafini, what then?"

"Surely he wouldn't—"

"Hold your tongue! What can you know of such things?" Maria stopped suddenly, her hands clamped to her mouth. A deep breath, striving for composure.

When she spoke again, her voice was calmer. "Go to bed, Philippa. It will be a long day for you too."

But before Philippa went to turn down the covers to the swansdown bed, she put her arm round Maria's shoulders with silent sympathy. And Maria held her hand for a moment, just a moment.

Then she went to bed.

CHAPTER 4

"Shhhh!"

"Well, hold it steady, can't you?"

His foot slipped again and he nearly fell back into the boat.

"Take your boots off," Marco snapped.

Gerain saw the sense in it. Barefooted, he tried again, feeling with his toes in his efforts to find the ledge Marco had described. The rope over his shoulder kept swinging forward and getting in the way.

He swore and stepped back into the boat again.

"What is it now?" Marco hissed.

Gerain said nothing, retying the rope so that

he could slip it over his head. Not for the first time that evening, he thought unkindly of his companion.

"You'll find it easy," Marco had said on the way out across the Bay of Stars. "Come on boy, you'll have no trouble . . . I've trained you for this, you'll manage." He had tilted his hat back then, fixing Gerain with those dark, moody eyes. "Remember what's at stake," he'd said firmly, "and all will be well."

Gerain sighed. There were times when he wondered whether Marco really did know best. This was perilous, wobbling in the tiny skiff in the cold, inky black night beneath the walls of Rienzi. Slimy stone towered over them, a hundred metres of cold granite. There were patrols along the battlements, he knew. Soldiers, guards and who knew what else . . . He wasn't altogether sure whether the Fireflies existed, those ferocious, inferno dragons with which the Rustrians threatened their enemies, but he didn't want to find out. The Guard of Rienzi were more than enough to cope with. They were famed for their suicidal courage throughout the length of Maquerlia. They took an oath, he remembered hearing, to accept torture until death if ever the Rustrian Royal Family were dishonoured. . . .

And what Gerain and Marco were up to would

certainly be considered the worst dishonour possible.

They'd timed it so that Gerain would get there between the two watches of the night. He had to get up on that ledge *now*, it had to be now. . . .

And then, magically, the clouds over the moon parted for a moment, and he saw the ledge, all two fingers' width of it, running along the perimeter of the wall in front of him. Without a further word to Marco, he stepped up on to it, his hands feeling above his head for the parallel ledge.

A frantic moment's scrabble with his fingers and then he found it, and his fingers fastened to it like leeches. He hung there for a moment, until he was sure of his balance, and then began to move, edging his way along the wall.

Behind him he heard Marco's long, slow whisper, "Good . . ." And then he forgot all about the boat, all about Marco waiting there and the others back on the shore. Like a fly against a window, he was inching along the traverse which would lead him into the heart of the Castle.

Maria was not asleep. She was too miserable for sleep, too upset to settle. It kept running through her head that tomorrow it would all be over. She would be married to frog-faced Ferrian and she would be stuck here in Rienzi, in this grim stone maze filled with soldiers and guards and horrible fire monsters for the rest of her life. There would never be any way out of it, never any chance of seeing her beloved Lassan again. . . .

Unless he came to rescue her at the last minute.

This thought crept into Maria's mind easily, insidiously. If only she'd sent word to him . . . Lassan had said that he would come, if ever she needed him, and she surely needed him now.

Ever since she had arrived at Rienzi she had been impressed and overwhelmed by the ostentatious wealth, by the prospect of power beyond her wildest dreams. She would be ruling an empire, everyone (including her parents) would bow to her . . . But getting to know Ferrian had changed all that.

He was cruel. He had enjoyed her discomfiture. He had forced her to watch that poor little calf and those people burn to death. She'd nearly been sick, and he hadn't cared at all! Lassan would never have subjected her to that, he cared if a hair on her head was out of place!

Oh, if only he would come and get her out of this! She lay in bed, her eyes open against the dark, and imagined Lassan appearing in a puff of violet smoke in the middle of the wedding ceremony. He'd scoop her up. He'd swing from the chandeliers and whisk her out of the Chapel to where his men would be waiting. . . .

She did not pause to wonder who would create the violet smoke, or how Lassan would manage to get the three men who comprised his followers into the Castle. She was also not interested in how they would manage to get out of the Castle past the Guard and the Fireflies. This was all fantasy, after all. She preferred to dwell on what Lassan would say, the look in his eyes as he wound strong arms around her waist. She also spent some time imagining the expression on Ferrian's face as she was carried beyond his reach forever.

And so when she heard scrabbling outside her bedroom window and saw a face peering through the glass, she did not scream or call for the Guard. She was half expecting it.

She fell out of bed and rushed to the window. In a moment it was open and he was standing there in front of her.

She lit the candle by her bed with shaking hands. There was a way out, she could leave . . . Lassan had come, just as he promised. . . .

But this was a stranger, someone completely unknown to her. She hesitated. The stranger was tall and thin with a mop of black, rain-damped hair. He was ragged, and his bare feet left smudges of mud and slime on the carpet.

Not at all what she expected. What was Lassan playing at? She stepped back, reaching for her wrap. The man smelt of seaweed and sweat.

"Who are you? What are you doing here?"

For a moment the man said nothing. She couldn't see his face at all clearly by the light of a single candle.

"Speak up, can't you? Who sent you?"

"You're to come with me. We're getting you out of here."

She was too delighted to notice the knife in his hands.

"Oh, thank goodness! Where's Lassan? Why didn't he come himself?"

Again that pause. Then the man said, "He was held up. My name's Gerain. Are you ready to come with me?"

"Oh yes! Of course I'll come!" Not a moment's doubt. "Oh, thank goodness you're here! It's been so terrible—"

"There's a boat waiting," he said.

For a moment she was disconcerted. "What, down there?" She looked past him to the window.

"I've got a rope," he said, unnecessarily. It was

43

trailing all over the floor around his feet. "You won't fall."

She was not reassured. She stepped back. "But I don't really understand. Where *is* Lassan? What hold up?"

"On the road," the stranger said vaguely. "A rockfall. He couldn't get away. But he'll be waiting for you, on the mainland. . . ."

And then the curtain to the alcove was swung open and Philippa was there, her eyes watchful, her dressing-gown drawn tightly around her.

Maria said, "Philippa, pack my things, quickly now. Lassan's rescuing us, we can get away. . . ."

"Doesn't look much like Lassan to me."

"He's called Gerain, he's been sent by Lassan. Come on, let's go!"

"There's not much time," the stranger said. "And she's not coming." He was referring to Philippa.

"Of course she is, I don't go anywhere without—"

"No way. I can't get two women down that drop."

Maria stared. She was not used to being crossed. "I insist she comes with me!"

"You don't have to worry about me, Mr Whoever-you-are Gerain," said Philippa. "I can look after myself."

The stranger looked suddenly harassed, much

younger than Maria had at first thought. He was hardly any older than she was. . . .

"Come on," Philippa said. "What are we waiting for?"

There was a small delay when Maria announced that she intended to take all the Soprafinian state jewels with her. She could not possibly leave them here, it would be the height of irresponsibility. . . .

"But they're in the Keep!" said Philippa. "We'll never get them out and there isn't time!"

Maria was slightly consoled by the discovery of the Soprafinian sapphire ring in the pocket of the dress she'd worn that day. With determination she wrenched off the enormous diamond Ferrian had given her and left it on the dressing table.

She was getting out, she was going to be free! What did jewels matter? She would have to make do with this one reminder of her home. Besides, sapphires suited her much better than diamonds. . . .

Maria allowed Gerain to loop one end of the rope round her waist. He tied a complicated sort of knot and attached the other end to his belt. He was giving instructions to Philippa all the time, something about keeping her face to the wall, and not looking down.

He suddenly paused. "You're too small," he said to Philippa. "You'll never reach the ledge."

Philippa was much shorter than Maria, a scrawny little dab, Maria always thought.

"You'll have to stay here," he said. His dark eyes were unhappy but determined. "You have to hold on to the ledge above, there's no other way."

Philippa wasn't listening. She was leaning out of the window, examining the wall's surface.

Maria said again, "Well, I'm not going without her. I never go anywhere without her. She's mine, she belongs to me, she goes *everywhere* with me!"

"Do you want to get out of here?" Gerain sounded suddenly fierce. "She'll fall. She'll kill herself. It can't be done." But even as he was speaking, Philippa was out of the window, her head disappearing over the sill.

Maria and the stranger ran to the window, looking down. They could just make her out, moving slowly and surely across the surface of the wall.

"Her fingers are small, perhaps she can find cracks . . ." Maria's voice trailed off. The wall looked smooth to her, smooth and slippery as glass.

"Come on," Gerain said. "Over the side with you. The first ledge is twenty metres down. I'll

lower you slowly. You'll find it, don't worry . . .
The other ledge is two metres beneath it. Hang
on when you get there and pull twice on the
rope when you feel steady. Wait for me. You're
tall enough, you'll reach it all right . . . Remember, not a sound. The boat's over on the other
side of the tower."

That descent, being swung over the dark
waters of the bay, was the most unpleasant
experience of Maria's sheltered life. She kept
hitting the wall, and the wind was whipping up
her hair so that she couldn't see. She hated
hanging there, helplessly, completely at the
mercy of this lanky, shabby looking boy. The
surface of the water was gleaming now in the
moonlight, and she could see no sign whatso-
ever of the two ledges. She supposed that
Philippa must be further over, managing somehow or other, but she didn't dare look.

Suddenly the descent stopped. Distractedly,
she searched the damp dark rock face and saw,
incredulously, the ledge.

No more than two fingers'-breadth wide.

He was mad! How could she possibly. . . ?
And then her feet banged against the wall and
snagged there, and she knew that she had
found the other ledge. A wild scrabble with her
fingers and then flooding relief as she realized
that the ledge was shaped like a drain. She

could hook her fingertips over it, and it was possible. . . .

The rope round her waist went slack, and she was alone, clinging to the wall, her breath in slight gasps, really very frightened.

"Lady?" Philippa's voice, over to her right. "This way. Carefully now, it's quite safe—"

Quite safe! In the pitch black, suspended above black water which for all she knew was filled with crocodiles and sharks and minskies . . . But she was moving, it was possible . . . She started inching slowly along against the foul, dark stone.

Surely Lassan could have managed it all better than this . . . But at least he had come.

She was getting out of Rienzi, away from Ferrian. She was free! She couldn't wait to see her lover again.

$\mathcal{T}$he boat was ridiculous. A smelly, dirty little skiff. Philippa was surprised. None of this was in Lassan Legrenzi's style. Not this embarrassed young man, not this ancient boat. The other man waiting there had been impatient and cross. Gerain introduced him as Marco.

"Hurry up and get in," he said. "The patrol will be out again in three minutes. Do you want to be discovered?"

"At least it's still raining," said Gerain. "No Fireflies tonight. Keep down, ladies. You don't want to get wet."

Maria crouched in the bottom of the boat with

Philippa, and Gerain covered them with a coarse blanket. It smelt of fish.

"Be very quiet," said Marco. "The Guard will be out on the battlements again by now."

With muffled oars, the boat began to move silently through the night.

Maria was pale with fury by the time they reached shore. Under the blanket Philippa did her best to keep her quiet but it was hard work. Maria complained of the cold, of the discomfort, of the discourtesy, of everything.

She seemed to have forgotten that she had wanted to escape. And when a small group of people on the shore approached with half-covered lanterns, and Philippa realized that Lassan was not among them she began to feel even colder. This wasn't right, this wasn't how Lassan operated. At her side, she heard Maria take a deep breath. They were going to have a tantrum if they were lucky, full scale hysteria if not. . . .

"Where is Lord Lassan?" Maria's voice, high-pitched with tension and anger, cut through the wind.

"He's been delayed. I told you." Gerain was surrounded by people patting his back, giving him congratulations. Philippa's hands clenched. This wasn't right, not right at all. No one was wearing Soprafinian livery, no one was bowing or making a fuss of the Princess Maria. Where were the deferential ambassadors, the hushed voices, the red carpet? These people were behaving as if Maria didn't matter at all.

As Maria's personal servant, Philippa had lived with Maria twenty-four hours a day. She tasted all Maria's food and drink, slept in Maria's dressing room, accompanied Maria through all the interminable and elaborate ceremonies that made up court life.

She had even been present during those dreary interviews between Maria and her parents, Gregor and Olivia of Soprafini. And although Maria's parents had been cold and withdrawn, although Maria had been allowed no friends at the court (there being no one of a similar rank), still no one had ever *ignored* her before.

Here, standing on that cold and lonely beach, it was as if the heiress to the Soprafinian throne was of no greater importance than her unremarkable servant.

It was as if Maria Soprafini hardly existed at all.

"This way. Come on." Someone had handed them cloaks, someone else had brought forward one of those sturdy mountain ponies that the common people rode.

"You want me to get on that? Are you *mad*?" Maria's eyes were flashing bright enough to compete with the outsize sapphire on her hand.

Philippa caught a glimpse of steel, heard the rasp of a scabbard. She swallowed and touched Maria's arm. "Forgive me, lady," she said. "I think you should do as directed."

"I am the Princess Maria! No one directs me!"

"We're still very close to Rienzi, lady," Gerain said. He looked distracted, uneasy. His eyes met Philippa's and she saw mute apology in them. "And this is all Rustrian territory. We are still in great danger. I think we should concentrate on getting away from here as quickly as possible."

"Do as you're told," Marco recommended. "This is neither the time or place for an argument."

Maria glared at him.

"If they let the Fireflies out after us," said Marco, calculatingly, "we won't stand a chance."

It was enough. Without another word, Maria swung herself up on to the pony's back and sat there staring stonily ahead. Thank God for Soprafinian training, thought Philippa, scrambling up on the back of her own pony. Those interminable hunting parties. At least Maria should be able to handle a short ride.

* * *

52

But it wasn't a short ride. It went on all night, winding through the boggy marsh land that surrounded the Bay of Stars. The ponies' hooves squelched in the mud and there was a damp, raw smell of marsh gas. It began to drizzle shortly after midnight, and the water soaked through their cloaks, soaked through to the bone, it seemed. Eventually their path began to rise as they approached the more undulating countryside of western Rustria, and they left the bog behind.

They were now in a land of lakes and rivers. There were bridges to cross, fords to wade through, all in pitch darkness. Once their path took them round the back of a vast waterfall and in the dark the ponies' hooves scraped and slithered.

By sunrise, some six hours later, Maria's back was still ram-rod straight, but Philippa could see her knuckles shining whitely with strain. Her own back and thighs were on fire although she was still shivering with cold and damp. Maria must be feeling the same. Her silence wouldn't last long. Soon, Soprafini pride would give way and the Princess Maria would start demanding attention.

They could see the track quite clearly now. It rose steeply in front of them, following the banks of a fast-running river. Marco raised his arm and pointed to an overhanging rock far above. Philippa heard the word "breakfast" and with a sinking heart estimated a further two hours' ride.

Maria reined in her pony. "I wish for refreshment now," she said clearly.

"Don't be stupid." Gerain turned and took hold of her reins. He gave a brief tug and the pony began to move again. "The Rustrians will have found out that you're gone by now. They'll have the Fireflies out soon. We have to get to the boats as soon as possible. There's no time to lose. We won't have a chance otherwise."

"Ten minutes will make no difference." Maria looked down her nose at him and hauled hard on her reins. The pony stamped.

"Look. Here you are." Gerain handed a greasy package and a battered leather flagon out to her. "You can eat this on the way."

She stared at it in disbelief. "Have you quite forgotten who I am? Do you truly imagine this—" she knocked it out of his hand, "a suitable repast for a royal princess?"

The men behind them were muttering at the hold-up. Marco had turned back from the front of the procession to see what was going on. Philippa slipped off her pony, meaning to retrieve the food from the dust. She was very hungry.

A large, sweaty hand closed over her shoulder. She felt a sharp pricking at her neck, and tried to pull herself away.

A thudding blow to the side of her head left her ears ringing. She was dimly aware of Maria's voice, outraged and emphatic. And then Marco said, and she hardly recognized his voice, "Remount. Don't *ever* try that again."

"How dare you? We're not your prisoners!" Maria shouted.

"And that's where you're mistaken, Princess Maria. That's exactly what you are." Marco smiled unpleasantly.

"You're not from Lord Lassan!" Philippa flared.

"Right first time."

She swung round to Gerain. They had trusted him! "Who are you? What do you want?"

Gerain would not look at her. "Just keep quiet and you'll come to no harm. We don't want any trouble—"

"No trouble!" Maria was white with fury. "This is a kidnap! You seize the future Queen of Rustria, and think there will be *no trouble*? Are you entirely mad?"

"What's the hold-up?" Another man had ridden up.

"Our – hostages – have just become aware of their status," said Marco.

The other man, dressed in dark brown robes, sighed. "I suppose we'd better tie them on, gag them or something—"

"Who *are* you?" Philippa stared from face to face, looking for clues. "What do you want with us?"

They were all dark, like she was herself. Small limbed, graceful, apart from the bean-pole that was Gerain. Wavy black hair, left long or tied back. Very unlike the rigid military style of the Rustrians, or the more foppish, elaborate artifice of the Soprafini.

"Barusi . . ." she breathed. "That's who you are. . . ."

"*What?*" Maria virtually shrieked. "Barusi? But they're outlaws!"

"Well, they're not precisely acting within the law now, are they?" Philippa said shortly.

"Shut up." Marco frowned at them. "We'll stop at the overhang. You can continue as you are, if you give us an undertaking to make no attempt to escape. Or we can tie you on. Take your choice."

In the end Maria and Philippa rode quietly in their place in the line, and only Philippa saw the tears streaking down Maria's cheeks.

The path wound round beneath the overhang and up on to a high plateau. Other mountains rose higher yet, tipped with snow, to the east. But ahead of them a wide lake stretched far over the horizon, cool and calm in the midday sun. It seemed very quiet, but high overhead a lark trilled. A family of ducks squabbled in the reeds, a moorhen trod delicately over the bank. In the distance, large white birds glided gracefully. Philippa didn't know whether they were geese or swans.

"What now?" Maria's voice was wavering. "Can we rest now?"

"In a moment." Gerain had not even looked at her. Instead he was watching Marco with the other men from the head of the column dismount and begin to pick their way over the rocks at the end of the lake. The overhang rock had been only one of many, clustered at one end of the lake.

A cloud ran over the sun. Philippa felt suddenly cold, suddenly sick and frightened again. As one, all the birds, the ducks and geese and swans suddenly lifted into the air, their wings beating against the chill air.

There were six men, including Marco. She noticed for the first time that they all wore the same drab brown cloaks over breeches and jerkins. They were standing in a semicircle facing the lake. Their hands were held out at waist-level, strong fingers pointing to the ground, slightly curved. They look like claws, thought Philippa. Like claws, or talons. . . .

Marco started it, intoning a deep low note. It vibrated strangely over the lake and Philippa saw the surface of the water shiver. One by one the other men joined in, building up a discordant harmony that unsettled the ear, disturbing the stomach.

It was horrible. Philippa thought she was going to be sick. The sound went on, getting stronger and louder. She lifted her hands to block her ears.

And then the surface of the ground began to shiver too, and the rocks were trembling, suddenly animated, possessed . . . And then one overbalanced and began to tumble over the edge of the plateau. It knocked against other rocks and the avalanche grew.

The lake surface shifted, rippled, and a regular pattern of small waves began to build. And when the rocks fell, the water followed close behind. In a mass, part of the lake started to slip and slide down the mountainside, rocks and water all mixed together, rushing to fall in a great curtain to the ground below.

"What are you doing, what are you doing?" Maria was shouting, half-screaming to be heard over the appalling noise of falling water and rock.

Gerain did not attempt to answer. He took

her arm and pointed far over the countryside beneath them.

And she saw in the distance, far along the track they had just left, a band of soldiers, armour gleaming faintly in the distance. Just behind them, sparking in uneven flares, the Fireflies in their strange watery-framed cages screamed like a great wind, wild to satisfy their appalling hunger.

The avalanche of rocks and water soon settled into a steady stream, filling the high sides of the track with an impassable torrent.

Marco and the others had stopped their singing and gradually the flow of water ceased. Enough rock had fallen to block the road. They had achieved their aim. No one would be able to follow their trail for a very long time. And the water still cascading down the mountainside would hold off the Rustrian army and the Fireflies.

"Now," said Gerain, slipping from his horse. "Breakfast, my lady? A little something. . . ?"

Maria was staring at the foaming river rushing down the mountainside. She was very pale. She leaned forward, her hand reaching out to Philippa.

"Oh, Philippa," she said, her voice little more than a whisper. "What have I *done*?"

CHAPTER 6

"Lady, it's not your fault—"

"I went with that man without thinking!" She pressed her palms to the sides of her face. "I ran out, and now whatever peace there might have been will be lost! The Rustrians may even attack Soprafini, Ferrian has more or less promised that they will, and he'll use those awful Fireflies – and it will all be my fault! I ran out!" There were tears streaming down her face.

"You couldn't have known—"

"I *should* have known! Of all people! But even if these – terrorists – had come from Lassan, even if we were with him now, it would have been no better! The whole safety of my country rested in *me*! They were relying on *me* to keep the Rustrians from attacking!"

There was little Philippa could say. She doubted very much that Maria's marriage to Ferrian would really have held back the Rustrians' expansion. Not since that visit to the Menagerie. Ferrian had been quite clear about the Rustrians' need for new territory. The Fire-flies needed feeding, and Ferrian would do anything to satisfy his pets. The marriage to Maria would count for nothing. It was throwing a straw in the face of a hurricane. Nothing was going to stop the Rustrians.

She thought that, quite possibly, Ferrian was mad. His eyes were more than cruel, there was a streak of lunatic recklessness there. She had never met Ferrian's father, King Ferdinand, who had not even bothered to get to know his future daughter-in-law. That alone made Philippa realize that the marriage was not an important event in Rienzi, that Maria was not regarded as a person of consequence.

Maria herself had noticed nothing. She had been too caught up in the preparations for the marriage to notice this lack of basic courtesy. She would not have complained, even if she *had* noticed it. Maria had always known that she was to marry Ferrian. She was to be a living pledge of friendship between the two nations, like the dam which had been built across the Ere.

The dam was a bridge between the two countries, its construction an act of trust, a celebration of the alliance.

But since Philippa and Maria had arrived in Rienzi, especially since seeing the Fireflies in action, Philippa had come to think differently. The Soprafinians were terribly at risk. Their army, although highly trained and efficient, was small: they had no machines, no artillery. They were even proud of their lack of military equipment. We don't get our hands dirty, it implied. We are delicate, cultured, civilized. . . .

But the Rustrians were predatory. Their economy demanded it; more urgently, the Fireflies demanded it. Marriage to Maria was just — a gloss, icing over a poisoned cake.

Philippa tried to discuss this with Maria as they waited by the side of the lake. They were eating bread and cheese and onions given to them by Gerain, and Philippa watched her mistress warily, waiting for the inevitable complaints. But Maria was now pale with worry, saying little, her hands restlessly twining together.

"My lady?" Philippa asked at length. "Have you had enough?" Maria had eaten next to nothing.

"Oh, Philippa. What are we going to do?"

"We'll have to wait and see what their plans are. I suppose they'll demand a ransom or something—"

"Why don't you ask them? I expect they'll let you in on it."

"My lady! What do you mean?"

"Well, look at you," Maria went on unhappily. "You're small and dark and thin . . . You might even be one of these – kidnappers – you might even be in league with them! How should I know?"

"My lady, I am not!" Philippa was on her feet, very distressed. "On my honour, I know nothing of these people!"

"But it's possible, isn't it? You could be Barusi, why not?" Maria's blue eyes considered the resemblances between her servant and kidnappers. "You look just like them. That dark hair, that small, feeble physique. I wouldn't be at all surprised if you were an aquemancer too. I saw the way they made that avalanche happen, that was aquemancy. Water-magic!" She spat the words in disgust. "And I've seen you, staring into dirty puddles all the time. You're always sneaking off to do it, don't think I haven't seen you. You've got aquemancy in your blood—"

"My lady, no!" Philippa was aghast. She had no idea that Maria had noticed this much.

"And the way you climbed that wall," went on Maria, relentlessly. "That's geomancy, you don't have to tell me. Geomancers can always climb anything made of rock or stone, everyone knows that. Breeding will out, after all. Blood tells, even blood tainted with magic will tell." She paused. "I am of royal blood, of course. I understand the importance of such things. You are Barusi, you can probably see visions in water, you can almost certainly make stone move. All those horrible tricks. This is probably all because of you."

This was dreadfully unfair but Philippa knew why Maria was hitting out. Maria was feeling guilty, and Philippa was the only available target.

And there was some truth in it, after all.

"No, my lady, I assure you," she said, trying to sound calm. "I was taken from one of the mountain tribes, you know that!"

"And where else do the Barusi live? Tell me that." Maria was too miserable to look pleased with herself. "I thought you were loyal!"

"My lady, I had nothing to do with this!"

"That she didn't." Gerain had approached while they were talking. He was looking tired and upset. "She's not one of us, your Highness. It's not her fault."

Maria turned her attention to Gerain, studying

the serious face with its dark eyes and straight mouth. It had honesty stamped all over it.

He towered over them both, even though Maria was taller than average. His legs looked too long for his body, but his hands were graceful and well made. There was nothing in his appearance to revolt, apart from his ragged clothes.

Gerain ignored Maria's scrutiny. He said patiently, "If you've finished, it's time to be moving on again."

"I cannot possibly ride another step," said Maria. "I must rest."

"You won't need horses now."

A small fleet of boats was approaching them from the far side of the lake. They glided silently over the water with neither sail nor oar.

"How do they move?" whispered Philippa, disconcerted by this. And then she heard the singing, the same low, monotonous tones that had caused the rocks beneath their feet to tremble.

In the helm of each boat a child sat, singing to something below the surface of the water. As the boats came closer, Philippa saw what it was.

Each boat was being towed by a large aquatic animal, something sinuously winding through the water. The creatures were roughly two metres in length, but it was difficult to see them clearly, as they kept well below the surface of the water. Philippa could only just see the harness strapped to the creatures' furry backs, the light chain which ran to the prow of each boat.

"Arethusans," she breathed. "I've heard about them—" And although Philippa was deeply frightened by this kidnapping, deeply worried about Maria, a thrill of delight ran through her.

Arethusans were part of folk mythology, something almost too good to be true, something magic. Although there were no magicians in Soprafini, neither pyromancers nor aquemancers, everyone had heard of the arethusans, those mysterious water creatures. Philippa thought they had been wiped out long ago, or that they only lived beyond the great sea. Certainly she had never seen one before.

They lived in partnership with certain favoured people, towing their boats, catching smaller fish, taking messages, giving rides to their children, so the legends said. They were not domesticated, as such. They lived in shoals far out in the centre of the lakes and only came to the shore, to their human friends, when they chose. . . .

There was something so graceful in these old stories. Philippa's favourite was about a young girl who fell in love with an arethusan and chose to live with him under the sea. Philippa, the servant who had neither freedom nor family, loved everything about this story. To swim in the wide seas with someone who loved you, to follow the currents and the tides and explore everywhere, without restraint.

She thought, the Barusi cannot be *all* bad, not if arethusans live with them.

But when she crouched down by the lakeside to look closer, she saw that these creatures seemed out of condition, sick or exhausted. Through the clear water their brilliant green eyes appeared cloudy, and there were occasional areas of dull, greasy skin showing in patches on the silver-grey pelt.

"What's wrong with them?" she asked Gerain. A flicker of emotion crossed his face.

"They're old," he said. "That's all. They're old, and there are no young to take their place. These are the last."

"The last? Oh, no." To find that arethusans really existed and then to discover that these were the last was almost too painful.

"Oh, yes," Gerain said grimly. "And this is the reason why you're here now."

"What do you mean?" He had Maria's full attention now, but there was no time for further talk. Less than gently they were handed into one of the boats by Marco. Gerain was instructed to get into another.

The child, a boy, at the prow began to sing softly and the girls' boat quietly left the shore, cutting through the undisturbed surface of the lake.

Philippa saw the ducks settle again in the reeds, the moorhens return to their haunts. She was about to point out to Maria the swans over on their right, but it would have been a waste of time.

Exhausted by the long night and too much emotion, Maria was asleep.

Philippa lay back against the rough blankets which lined the bottom of the boat and considered their position. She could recognize that Maria's suspicions had their roots in Maria's own fear and dismay. She would probably have forgotten all about it by the time she awoke. For all her faults, Maria wasn't one to sulk. And soon, with any luck, they would be rescued from these rebels.

And yet, did they want to be rescued? She thought of what life in Rustria would be like, life living in Rienzi, in close contact with Ferrian and his brutish servants.

She shuddered.

She knew that the avalanche would not hold off pursuit for long. Already the Rustrians were out in force looking for them. Messages would be sent to Soprafini and then no doubt Maria's father would call out the troops to scour the countryside from the south-west. She knew that within hours they would probably be back in the hands of the Rustrians.

"Why on earth are you doing this?" she asked Marco, who sat behind them, a sharp knife laid across his knees.

He smiled slightly, contemptuously.

"You must know it's hopeless. There's no possible way you can get away with this."

"Be quiet. You're putting off the singer." And indeed, the song from the boy in the front of the boat had hesitated and with it their motion.

Philippa looked more curiously at the singer. He was slight, dark like all the other Barusi, his eyebrows almost meeting across the centre of his forehead. He was wearing dark blue, coarse-woven cloth, but unlike the older men he carried no weapon. She noticed, with a shock, that there was a web of skin between each of his fingers.

There were scars on her own hands, where the webbing had been cut. Did all the Barusi have webbed hands? Did that make *her* a Barusi, too?

She could just see Gerain in the boat in front. He was leaning against the side of the boat, his face turned away from them. His tall, lanky figure looked uncomfortably cramped, but his long-fingered hands, lying on his knees were relaxed. No webbing there, no scars either. So, not everyone.

She knew nothing about her parents. No one had told her where she came from. She was just one of the mountain children, brought into Soprafini as slaves. She had no keepsake, no memory or clue to her past.

She could be Barusi. Or Rustrian, or Brican or Melshan; any of the countries in Maquerlia.

In some ways it gave her a strange freedom. She need not be limited by Soprafinian customs or boundaries. But this freedom was very far from a physical fact: as a slave, she could not even call her name her own. Everything about her, her clothes, her education, her food, belonged to someone else.

Her thoughts were her own, that and her secret. Philippa held them fiercely private, unwilling to share with anyone.

Who was there to share with, anyway? Maria Soprafini? With some bitterness, Philippa saw her mistress snuggle more deeply into the blankets. Maria never found it hard to sleep, never worried about her past or her inheritance. Her identity was secure, her future assured.

Or it had been. Philippa realized, looking round, that there were no women there. Why not? And then she wondered for a moment how Maria would have managed alone amongst these people, if Philippa had not insisted on coming too. Whether the tantrums and the tears would have led to violence on the part of their captors.

Not Gerain, she thought. He would never have let it go that far. She saw kindness in his dark eyes, although he was too much under the sway of that man Marco. . . .

But Maria would have been ruined, Philippa realized, which ever way it had gone. Even if she'd managed to escape. The marriage with Ferrian of Rustria would never take place, not after the bride-to-be had spent hours alone in the company of men. Her reputation, even as heiress to Soprafini, would never recover. The marriage treaty between the Rustrians and the Soprafini would never be signed.

The sun was high in the sky, and although Philippa had been awake all night, still she could not sleep. Her thoughts fretted around what might happen. She was anxious, always had been. An orphan child taken into slavedom in the Palace of Soprafini had to learn caution, had to learn not to panic when things went wrong.

Panic made you vulnerable, made you stupid. You made things worse with unplanned actions.

She remembered the day she had broken a glass while washing up. She could only have been five or six, because it was during those very early days with Maria, when she still spent time at kitchen duties.

She had crashed the glass against the underside of the tap, and the frail shards had sparkled in the soapy water. Half-sobbing, she had searched through the sink until she had found all the bits. Without thinking, she had pushed them up inside the gathered fullness of her sleeve, a stupid thing to do. But someone had pushed her and she had fallen . . . The blood had given away her clumsiness. The beating had left no scars, but her forearm was streaked with shiny skin even now, ten years later. Hide your mistakes immediately, she had learned. Put the blame on others, divert attention away from yourself. Destroy the evidence before you were caught. . . .

She couldn't think of any way to conceal her part in this kidnap. Why didn't you raise the alarm, they would ask her? Are you one of them, had you *known* they were coming?

She hadn't known that. But she was indeed one of them, there was no way round that.

They used aquemancy and so did she.

For as long as she could remember, Philippa

had been fascinated by water. Nothing to do with swimming or drinking it. She just wanted to watch it, to see how light altered the shine of its surface. She could be distracted from her work for hours by the pattern of rain against a window. And water in a lily-pool drew her like a magnet, drew her to stop and stand and stare until sharply recalled to her duties.

She had been thirteen when she had realized something else. That the pictures she saw in water were not merely reflections.

She would watch, entranced, as a thousand scenes flashed dimly over the gleaming surfaces. She saw people laugh and sing somewhere far out in the country, somewhere among rocky, precipitous scenery. Quite unlike the low valleys of the Soprafini. They wore long cloaks, dark colours, but their faces laughed, their eyes sparkled.

She wondered who they were. Sometimes she thought that these pictures must be scenes from her own past, glimpses caught from her own memory of the time before she was taken to work in the Palace of Soprafini. She could remember nothing of her life then.

Sometimes, if she were truly relaxed and on her own at the top of one of the towers, if she then held water between her own hands, she would sometimes see something else. Dreams, visions . . . scenes from somewhere she definitely did not know, did not recognize. Her memory had never contained such wide open spaces, such soaring mountains and empty skies.

She had never called her talent aquemancy. Aquemancy, like boreomancy, pyromancy and geomancy, was one of the four black arts. Illegal in Soprafini, used only in Ferrian's workshops in Rustria. It was just like dreaming, to Philippa, something private she did not want to share with anyone else.

It was very quiet, apart from the slight murmur of the singer's droning song, the slight swish of the boat against water. She moved forward, careful not to disturb Maria, and looked over the edge at the arethusan below. In the depths she saw the great creature waver softly as its muscles rippled. It seemed half veiled and then she realized that its fur was long, wafting around it, disguising its true shape.

She felt the eyes of the singing boy on her and looked up. His song did not cease but there was kindness in his gaze, sympathy and some curiosity.

She felt strangely like crying. She found herself yawning and realized that at last she would be able to sleep. She settled herself back in the boat near to Maria and closed her eyes.

They made no stop that day, nor the following night. The arethusans towed the boats across a chain of lakes, dotted with islands, surrounded and interspersed by vast, craggy mountains. It was entirely deserted: no crofts, no shelter even for sheep. Indeed, Philippa saw no other living creatures at all apart from birds and fish. They were traversing a treeless land, high above the comfortable plains and valleys she knew.

It became very cold as night approached. Maria had woken and was complaining once more. She said she was hungry, but refused the Barusi's food. "Too rough," she moaned. "I am delicate, must have white cakes, a little fruit, perhaps steamed fish . . . Philippa, make me some fruit pilaff, some cow's milk perhaps. . . ."

But there was only coarse bread and dry cheese and water to drink. "I am sick, do you want me to die?" Maria pushed the food away.

"You will not die." Gerain spoke patiently. Every now and then the boats put in to the side, to allow the arethusans to rest, their singer had explained, and everyone disembarked to stretch their legs. Gerain had wandered over with another greasy package of food. "Nothing will happen, we are just – holding on to you for a while. Until certain conditions are met."

"What conditions?" Watching carefully, Philippa saw Gerain's dark eyes flicker again. "Why won't you tell us?"

"It is of no concern to you."

"It's of every concern!"

But he just shook his head and handed them back into their boat. They glided on through the night, and Philippa drifted in and out of sleep. She found it curiously restful to be rocked in this little boat, taken far away from everything she had ever known. And yet she knew that this was only an interlude, an interruption, before the action began. Neither she nor Maria knew what was at stake.

Next morning they were passing very swiftly along a narrow stretch of water. Imperceptibly, the chain of lakes had given way to a river. Steep sides of rock surrounded them, and a strong current whisked them along. The arethusans were hardly having to work at all. But Philippa saw that their singer was still murmuring, his eyes watchful, a faint frown of concentration on his face as he balanced their movement against the pull of the current.

Very quiet at first, and then growing until they could hardly hear each other talk, a roaring sound filled the gorge as it twisted through the mountains. The boats were being drawn very swiftly now between the blank walls of rock.

Maria uttered a faint scream as the boat rocked and dipped in the violent water. Both girls were clutching the sides of the boat in terror as the speed increased.

"I don't like this!" Maria wailed. "I'm going to be sick, you'll have to stop, stop the boat—"

"Be quiet!" Marco shouted. "We must not disturb the singer!"

And then, as the boat turned round another bend in the gorge the river dropped away in front of them. There was only air ahead of them, empty clean air.

The river disappeared over the edge of a vast precipice.

CHAPTER 7

"**H**old on!" shouted Gerain, and terrified as she was, Philippa saw the child singer lean forward and then, just at the moment when the boat balanced on the edge of the unseen drop, the singer loosed the chain that bound the arethusan to the boat.

And then the boat fell over the lip of rock, crashing almost vertically down through gallons of surging water and she could hardly breathe, hardly think. It seemed impossible that they should not be flung out of the bucking boat as it dipped this way and that between water and rock. They were all drenched over and over with freezing water. She saw Gerain's large wide hand clutching Maria's arm, and then realized that the singer was holding on to her as well.

The boats were rushing down something that was almost a waterfall, something much steeper than rapids. And a little way ahead, all Philippa could see through the leaping spray was the river, disappearing again in front of them, and a wide landscape of watery fields and mountains and lakes far, far away.

They were rushing towards another edge, and this one was different. No rapids this time, this was a true overhang, a classic waterfall. Hundreds of feet, thousands, and they would crash into a vortex of water and rock and they would all die. . . .

But the singer suddenly leaned forward and hooked the chain round the arethusan that had somehow managed to reappear beneath their boat and the great creature suddenly tugged them to one side.

They almost lost their grip on the frail wooden sides as the boat swerved and swayed and then suddenly, suddenly, Philippa saw a tiny bay, a small recess in the wild rock walls, a calm haven just short of the precipice.

The arethusan pulled them there, crossing the terrific drag of the water.

Gasping, soaked and breathless, the two

girls clung together. "Are they trying to kill us?" Maria cried. "Are they mad?"

Philippa saw the efficient way the Barusi moored their boats, the way they seemed to congratulate, to thank the arethusans. "They're not mad," she said. "Not at all. Come, my lady, it's only water, we'll soon have you warm and dry again. . . ."

"Oh Philippa, I want to go home!" Maria's hands were clutching her cloak. "I don't like this, I don't understand what's going on. What's going to happen to us?"

"I don't like this." Gerain was staring bleakly at Marco. They were sitting together in a cave just out of sight of the river. "This . . . isn't right. Using people as bargaining counters."

"It's an ancient custom." Marco shrugged. "Who are you to be so choosy? Maria Soprafini is heiress to a kingdom run by feeble-minded idiots. Can't you tell?" Cruelly, he mimicked her. " 'I can't eat this, a little fruit, some steamed fish—' God, what a fool! Sad, don't you think? The family she proposes to marry into aren't much better. A bunch of ruthless, aggressive meat-heads. Why should we care about her?"

Gerain was looking increasingly uncomfortable. "She can't help the way she was brought up, any more than I can . . . And her servant, Philippa, is one of us."

"What? Just because she's small and dark and has green eyes? Come on, Gerain, you're not that naive!"

"It's more than that." And although he was beginning to doubt Marco and knew that he was laying himself open to Marco's derision and sarcasm, Gerain went on. Doggedly. He could never match Marco's quick-wittedness.

He reminded Marco about the way Philippa had climbed down the walls of Rienzi, the way she had been so enchanted by the arethusans. "She wasn't frightened," he said. "Not even when we went over the Drop. She didn't know what was happening, she gasped . . . but there was no panic there, no real loss of control."

"Probably too stupid to realize the danger."

"She's not like that!"

"So? It makes no difference."

"Well, what are we going to do with them then? What if the Soprafini do agree? Once we give up the hostages they'll come after us. You know that." Gerain was trying to sound calm and reasonable, but still he was pacing up and down the cavern. He'd never disagreed with Marco before, not like this.

"Didn't you think of that?" Marco was sitting with his knees drawn up against the wall.

Everyone else was drying off in another cavern a little further down the passage.

The knife between Marco's long fingers was sharp enough to slice hair, and that was what he was doing. He ran his fingers through greasy long, black curls and pulled out another, slicing at it methodically.

At length he sighed, putting the knife down. "Why all this concern, Gerain? Do you fancy one of them?"

"What? What's that got to do with it?" He stopped pacing, glaring at Marco, running his hand through his hair. "They're just girls, they haven't done anything!"

"Not to my taste, I must say. Too scrawny altogether. The blondie's got the temper of a wolverine and the other's nothing to write home about. Nothing there to excite, I'd have said."

"But this is all nothing to do with them. It's not their fault!"

"Not their fault that the Ere was dammed? Not their fault that the arethusans are dying?"

"For Heavens' sake!"

"It was Gregor of Soprafini who built that dam, Maria's father. Have you forgotten?" Marco was relentless. He always knew how to manipulate Gerain.

As usual, Gerain shut up. It always came back to this. The arethusans had always returned along the River Ere to the sea at regular intervals, ever since anyone could remember. There was an island off the coast, so it was said, where they brought up their young. No one knew for sure, no human had ever visited it.

But it was certain that there were no arethusan young now, not since the Soprafinians had dammed the river in their efforts to pacify Rustria. The River Ere now ran from the mountains down into a lake. The route to the sea was blocked, and the arethusans no longer had young. They were dying out.

And so Marco had conceived this daring plan to kidnap Maria. The price of her release would be the breaking of the dam. It had all seemed simple enough in the planning, a courageous and difficult feat. But now, now faced with Maria and Philippa, Gerain was beginning to see flaws in the plan.

He had just not considered what it would be like to take and trick and hold prisoner two other human beings. He was rather appalled at the way he had been swept along by Marco's plan.

It was not Maria who moved him. He thought her spoilt, ill-disciplined, a snob . . . but Philippa was different.

Nothing to write home about, Marco had said. It wasn't unfair. She was small, thin-chested like a boy, her hair an undistinguished brown. But her face was pointed and delicate, her eyes too big, green and wary as a cat's.

He saw worry and impatience in her face. She was so self-contained that he wondered if she ever laughed. The perfect servant, fussing around her mistress, never putting herself first. And in the back of his mind, he remembered the way she had handled that climb down the castle walls. Something more than competent there, he thought. Something that he recognized from his own experience.

He watched her all the time, and then listened to what Marco was saying.

"Don't get too fond, Gerain. Those girlies are probably not going to make it out to the sun again. . . ."

"*What?* What do you mean?"

Marco stood up, his dark eyes glancing away. "Well, we can't let them go, can we? Not after they've seen all this. I'm afraid I can't see much in the way of a future for our little princess and her serving maid."

"Are you out of your mind? Are you seriously suggesting we keep them prisoner for ever?"

"Something like that."

"What does the Council think about this?"

"Ah." Marco looked pensive. "I may – slightly – have misled you, Gerain. The Council does not actually know that we have taken Maria of Soprafini hostage—"

"They don't *know*? But I thought . . . You did this *without* authority?"

"Correction, Gerain. *We* did it without authority." Marco frowned. "You and me. We're in this together. I considered telling them. But you know what the Council's like, that bunch of elderly no-hopers. They never listen to anything *I* say. I felt it was time to take the matter into my own hands. They'll be glad enough when the arethusans are saved."

"But—" Gerain was stunned. He had assumed right from the start that this was Council business, that they'd undertaken this exploit with the full support of the Barusi Council of Aquemancers. Marco had let him think that this was a Council plan – he had deliberately *lied*!

This was all incomprehensible. "Why didn't you tell the Council?" His voice sounded thick and stupid.

"They wouldn't listen. They never understood me, never valued or appreciated what I could do. They left me powerless. But let me tell you this, Gerain. If we pull this one off, the Barusi will look to me to lead them from now on. No more of those interminable meetings. *I* shall make the decisions."

"What? You're out of your mind!" Gerain backed away from Marco. He felt as if he was looking at this man for the first time, as if he'd never known what Marco was really like.

"I'm not alone, Gerain. Remember that. I have friends here, friends who will be loyal to me unto death." He smiled suddenly, ironically. "I'm being practical, Gerain. Strictly practical." He jammed the knife into his belt.

Gerain stared at him. "I can't believe I'm hearing this! You must be mad!"

"Your trouble is that you never think, my lad. There's only one thing to remember. The arethusans are going to die, because of that Soprafinian dam. A year, two perhaps . . . that's all they've got left. Are you telling me that two spoilt city girls are worth the whole race of arethusans? Are you? Is that what you're saying?"

"There must be some other way! There has to be!"

"Find it, then, Gerain. If you're so clever. Find it."

Marco turned on his heel and left the cave, his cloak swirling behind him. Gerain scowled, and hit his fist twice against the rock. He was furious with himself. Why had he always trusted Marco? Why had he always relied on Marco to make the decisions, to run the show?

It was a familiar story. Marco had been appointed guardian to Gerain after the death of his parents. He had been father and mother, brother and sister, to the young boy.

Marco was also a powerful aquemancer, and Gerain had been impressed. Marco belonged to the Barusi Council of Aquemancers, and Gerain knew that everyone looked up to him, everyone relied on him.

Of course Gerain trusted Marco. No one had ever given him any reason not to. And so when Marco had told him about the Council's secret plan, he had been pleased and flattered to be involved. It had seemed reasonable enough, to hold Maria Soprafini for a while. Just until the dam was broken. . . .

But Marco had lied. This wasn't a Council plan at all. This was Marco's bid for power. He wanted to supplant the Council. . . .

Gerain shuddered. Did Marco actually care about the arethusans at all? Or did power come first? Sickeningly, the answer was staring him in the face. The quest to free the arethusans was a blind, a diversion. All Marco really cared about was destroying the Council.

How could he have been such a fool? How could he have been taken in?

The plight of the arethusans had blinded him. Gerain would have done anything, almost anything to save them. And Marco had taken advantage of his emotional muddle-headed stupidity!

And the girls! He had assumed that the girls would go free after the dam was destroyed, and that would be the end of it. He hadn't looked far enough, he hadn't *thought* of the consequences.

And then something else struck Gerain. *Something like that*, Marco had said. If they weren't going to keep the girls prisoner, what else did he mean?

Gerain's world was collapsing round him. For a moment he stood alone in the cave, and his hand fell to the hilt of his dagger. "Oh, no," he said, very softly. "Oh, no, not that."

They left the open air far behind. Once they'd dried out they all piled back into the boats and the arethusans were harnessed once more.

Then the descent into the heart of the mountain began. For long stretches, they were towed through dark tunnels, where the bats flew and strange rocks glimmered in the torchlight. Water dripped everywhere, and elongated stalactites hung from the ceilings. Sometimes it was like finding a path through a forest of hanging rock, interminably weaving in and out.

And then there were other passages where the water disappeared altogether, plunging through holes in the rocky floor. Then they had to negotiate ladders, ropes; long, cramped tunnels where they had to crawl on hands and knees, leading ever downwards. The arethusans always followed the water, down into deep pits where they could hear the rushing sound of other, deeper, rivers.

Their passage was lit only by rough torches carried by every fourth man. Maria complained every step of the way, with some reason. The going was very hard, the tunnels often littered with rockfalls or slippery with mud. Water dripped constantly from the roof. Threats had to be used more than once. Philippa, at her side, tried to offer encouragement, but it was difficult in all that gloom, surrounded by such hostile people. It was easier by far in the boats, when the presence of the arethusans seemed to defuse the threat of darkness and violence.

After some hours, hours which felt like days or weeks of crawling and climbing and clinging, Philippa realized that the passages were becoming wider and taller. They could stand upright at last. The torches were stuck into brackets on the walls. She heard a hubbub of noise from somewhere far ahead. People used this way often, she realized. And then, up ahead, the passage opened into a wide cavern, soaring hundreds of feet over the lake that lay before them.

To call it a lake did not do it justice. This was a vast expanse of water, an inland sea, so large that they could make out no details on its far side. Clusters of small lights flickered there, like villages on a far shore.

Noise assaulted them. They were standing on a balcony which jutted over a subterranean sea full of traffic. From the confusing light of thousands of torches and fires, Philippa knew a whole world existed here, in this immense underground cavern.

It was crowded with people, a city of people, all spread out over the water, in boats and barges and skiffs and gondolas. Thousands of small craft jostled for position, scudding across the open channels like so many coloured insects.

Men yelled at each other, children shouted and screamed and laughed. Just beneath them, a man was bellowing out his wares: eel pies, salamander sandwiches and shrimp sausages. Someone else nearby was singing, and then an argument started up between two men wanting to steer down a narrow tunnel at water-level. All this, just beneath their feet.

For a moment, confused by the noise and light, Philippa glanced away from the sea. Above her, the ceiling was lost in shadow, immensely far away. She could just make out that the walls were honeycombed with tunnels like the interior of a beehive. A million ways out, a maze with no map. At many of the openings hung a balcony, just like their own, with steps or ladders leading down to water-level. Others were black holes, leading who knew where.

"Boats again." Maria sounded depressed and exhausted.

"Look at this!" Philippa was astounded. "Did you ever think that such a place existed? All these people, living here—"

"And we never knew." Maria had caught something of Philippa's amazement. "We had no idea . . . my father told me that only remnants of the mountain tribes existed, that the Rustrians had wiped them out . . ." She paused. "But they were here, all the time, waiting and watching and planning. . . ."

Philippa was scanning the great cavern more carefully now. How to tell one tunnel from another? Her mind filed away shapes and shadows. If we have to make a run for it, she thought, we'll need to know the landmarks. But even as she tried to make sense of the patterns, she knew it was hopeless. This was too vast, too complicated and strange. They'd never find their way out again.

At the bottom of the steps another small skiff waited for them, this time paddled by one of the singers. Philippa couldn't see Gerain at first, and then realized that he was way ahead of them in a boat with Marco. She was aware that they were arguing although she could hear no words.

She could hear very little precisely, in all the noise. How could so many people live here, on water? She saw then that logs had been roped together to form floating platforms. These acted as walkways, and also separated the various lanes where small boats bobbed this way and that. Further out from the walls, great ornate barges were lit with braziers and chains of tiny lights. Traders yelled their wares, from boats and from kiosks on the platforms. Smoke, smelling of roast meat and charcoal and incense and oil lamps, clouded the air.

This was a floating market, Philippa realized. She saw people bartering fish, cloth, pots, vegetables . . . Where do they get them from, she wondered? Living here, underground, how can they grow anything? There were even tents showing the signs of the exotic arts, fortune-tellers, sorcerers, clairvoyants. All forbidden on pain of death in both Soprafini and Rustria.

She thought at first that no one was paying them any attention, but occasionally she noticed someone following the movement of their boat across the lake. A face would turn, and then the message would spread. She saw hands clench on swords, she saw the rigid expression on too many faces, a hurried movement, quickly suppressed.

The Barusi have hidden nothing from us, she thought with deepening despair. They haven't even bothered to blindfold us. This is an illegal and dangerous community: they're all outlaws and magicians. And yet they don't mind us seeing everything. No one's made any attempt at concealment.

She looked at the man paddling the skiff. His brows were straight, his mouth a tight thin line. It looked ruthless, almost cruel. She wondered where Gerain was, and realized that she had seen very little of him for quite some time. Has he abandoned us, she wondered? Doesn't he care? It seemed unlikely. He had been patient and kind to them during the ride, he had tried to get them food and warm clothes . . . And then another terrible thought struck her. Does he think we have no future? Does he know that we can never be allowed to leave here? Her hands suddenly clasped together.

She glanced across at Maria. She was trailing her hand through the dark water, watching the ripples in the flickering torchlight.

Philippa leant across. "Lady . . . we've got to get away. We have to escape—"

Maria glanced at her. "Nonsense. Ferrian will pay whatever ransom is required. Or my father. No one will allow harm to come to *me*."

"Lady, we've seen all their secret places now. We know where the outlaws live, they'll never let us go. They may keep us alive until Lake Ere is drained, or whatever it is they want, but we'll never get out of here."

"Resign yourselves then." The man with the paddle spoke over his shoulder to them. Philippa felt a cold shiver. How could he have heard their slight whispers over the noise and clamour of the market?

"You are with the Barusi, remember. And we live beneath the protection of stone, in a safe haven of water. We make our lives using geomancy and aquemancy. And we use water to judge, to divine, to tell us whatever we want to know . . ." The man stopped paddling for a moment, and with a flick of his wrist, scooped a handful of water from the sea. He held it out to them and they saw their own faces reflected back at them and clearly written on those faces was their doubt and fear.

"Yes," confirmed the man. "I can hear everything you say, caught and echoed back to me by these holy waters. You will never see the sun again, it is true. You will have to make your lives here within stone, forever and ever." His bleak, passionless voice ground on. "It could be worse. If you try to escape, you will be killed."

His fingers were webbed, like those of the boy singer. Another Barusi, with webbed hands, practising aquemancy.

These were Philippa's people. But not her friends.

CHAPTER 8

They were taken through part of the market, across to a dark and shadowy area of the great cavern. Philippa watched and observed and despaired. The size of it was beyond comprehension, the number of people everywhere terrifying. It was a warren, a maze, and even if they did manage to escape, they'd never find their way out again.

Maria had withdrawn into a depressed silence.

And then their boat turned away from the crowds and the bright lights, down one of the many tunnels back into the wall of stone. There was an immediate change of atmosphere. Rock enclosed them once more. They found themselves paddling through another dank channel, lit by infrequent torches. Only one other boat went with them. Gerain, she saw. And Marco.

The tunnel forked and they went left. Another fork, and they turned right. They passed a number of other tunnels, some better lit than others, some crowded with boats and people, others dark and deserted and full of strange echoes. It was down one of the blackest of holes that they were eventually taken, and only Philippa noticed the men stationed at the mouth of it, the men with long, shining knives and unsmiling eyes.

Gerain's boat stopped, and they saw his thin figure leap up on to a ledge. When their own boat halted, he helped them out. "You will be quite safe if you keep close to me," he said.

The two girls looked back towards the way they had come and saw only Marco, with one of those wicked looking knives. He motioned for them to follow Gerain.

Their choices, as ever, were limited. Maria took Philippa's hand, and followed Gerain. It was very dark, and difficult to make out where they were but at one stage Philippa was aware of a rushing sound of deep water running through rock. For a few paces their footsteps sounded against wood, not rock. A bridge, she thought. A bridge over another, fast-flowing river. And then Gerain struck a flint, and a torch flared into light.

They were all three of them in a large cave, cold and damp. Water ran down the walls. A few rugs and blankets lay in a heap in a corner. On a ledge Philippa saw a pitcher, a plate of fruit and bread and dry meat. And as she looked again, searching for some clue to their imprisonment, she heard a grating sound.

She swung round. The rickety wooden bridge had been drawn up on the other side of the tunnel. It had spanned a channel, over three metres in width. Gerain was standing there, on the other side, looking towards them.

The expression on his face was not comforting. Philippa ran forward.

"Stop!" he shouted. "Don't come any further! There are minskies in that ditch, you must go nowhere near it. . . ."

And horrified, looking down, she saw the sharp bright eyes of the minskies and the formidable double rows of teeth flashing in the fast-running water.

"We'll bring you food and water, you must not worry. And soon, once the message has gone through, you will be released. . . ."

"Liar!" said Philippa. "How can you let us go?"

He looked very white. "I swear it," he said.

"When this is done, you will go free."

And then he looked over his shoulder quickly as Marco came up to them. "We have to go now, to organize . . . your release," he said. "Remember, keep clear of that channel. Minskies can strip a human body to the bone in seconds."

Philippa stared after him, furious and helpless. "You . . . *louse*," she said under her breath. "Just you wait."

"Are they really minskies?" Maria was standing at her shoulder, her eyes enormous.

For answer, Philippa went over to the little pile of food and pulled apart a chicken leg. She tossed the flesh into the ditch and there was a flurry, a horrible chaotic mess of threshing fin and snapping teeth that proved the point.

"No paddling today," she said.

"Philippa . . . do you think he means it? Will they really let us go?"

Philippa considered her mistress. It was most unusual for Maria to be asking *her* questions. Somehow, imperceptibly, the balance of authority between them was altering. "Lady, I think they would be fools to let us go."

"They are fools to think they can get away with this."

They may not get away with it, thought Philippa, but we won't be here to see it.

"And anyway," said Maria, "*I* can't remember how we got here. All those tunnels, all those turns. They'd be quite safe, we'd never be able to give anything away."

"It would be enough to reveal that so many people live here, lady. Just think. The Rustrians, if not your own family, would scour every inch of these mountains, once they knew that so many Barusi still survive."

"What do they want with us? Why are they keeping us here?" Maria had pulled a cloak from the pile and now sat on one of the rugs, cuddled up in the coarse wool.

"Well, Barusi are considered traitors, of course. They may want some kind of political acknowledgment."

"I suppose so . . . It's rather mad, though, isn't it? A huge risk really, to kidnap a princess." She went over to the dish of fruit and chose an apple from it. "Anyway, who are the Barusi? I've never really understood why they are so hated by our people. What do they do, apart from kidnapping and extortion?"

Philippa sighed. The Court at Soprafini had sheltered its young princess, but servants were different. Philippa had picked up a great deal below stairs when she was off duty. She remembered stories told among the kitchen maids about the Barusi. They cast curses, the maids had said, with a thrilled giggle. They can send a curse along a stream of water so that it leaps up like a fountain and drowns the one who has offended. They can make people cry their eyes out. Literally. Alternatively, they can drain all the water from a person, so that the flesh dries out and falls to desiccated dust in an instant.

They can cause mountains to crack and stones to fall from heaven.

Philippa had listened round-eyed to such stories, but had been inclined to dismiss most of them. But one thing was clear.

"They are magicians, my lady," she said. "That's what's wrong. They're aquemancers and geomancers. And as you know, it's illegal in Soprafini. They use horoscopes, herbal medicines, the cards . . . all the fortune-telling arts. Your ladyship's parents loathe such things. It's the same in Rustria. Prince Ferrian works with pyromancers but I don't suppose anyone else is allowed to. It's too underhand, too slippery to make laws or rules for, or something. Magic is not allowed, at least for the common people. It's reckoned . . . dangerous."

She thought of that avalanche of rock and water and shivered. *That* was real power, more dangerous than weapons or armies. "Not everyone can do it, of course. And people who can't get jealous and frightened. That's the main part of it."

She paused, remembering something else. "The other thing is that the Barusi fought against the building of that dam, the one blocking the River Ere. We crossed it on the way here, remember? There were all those stories about how they tried to hold up the work . . . There was a lot of trouble. It's why the Barusi were banished from Soprafini, and from Rustria. I thought only a few were left, just a few hundred perhaps. They live in the mountains, we always knew that much."

"Where *you* come from," said Maria accusingly. She was frowning.

Philippa sighed. "Well, my lady, perhaps I am Barusi, too, but I remember nothing of my past life . . . I had no idea so many of them were left, I had no idea of all this. . . ."

"I shall smash it all. I shall get my father to clear this place, to take prisoner everyone involved in this. I shall destroy that awful man Marco and stupid Gerain—"

"Gerain may be our only hope." Philippa spoke softly.

"What do you mean?"

"He swore that he would see us safe—"

"He's a fool." Maria spoke dismissively. "Anyway, you can't believe the word of a kidnapper."

"It's the only chance we've got, lady." Philippa sat down on the rug next to Maria. "I think we may *have* to trust him."

"Nonsense. Why do you always contradict me? Someone will come, of course they will. We will be rescued." Maria glared at Philippa.

Philippa sighed. "Nobody knows this place exists," she said gently.

For a moment it looked as if Maria was going to start shouting. But instead she turned away from Philippa and started flipping bits of stone into the channel of minskies.

Teeth gnashed and clashed around their prison.

CHAPTER 9

In another cave, some distance from the two girls, Marco was summoned to a meeting by the Barusi Council of Aquemancers and Geomancers.

There were thirteen of them, led by Zarah, a grim-faced woman who rarely smiled. Her iron-grey hair was scraped back from her face, her hands were gnarled and twisted with age. Marco, who knew her well, saw immediately that she was furious.

"We have been told that you have kidnapped Princess Maria of Soprafini and her serving maid. We would like to know your reason for this act of extraordinary lunacy." Zarah, although angry, spoke with cold composure. "Whatever gave you the idea that you could act like terrorists?"

Marco snarled, "The arethusans are dying! Someone had to act!"

"You are a dangerous and stupid man." She was severe.

"You wouldn't let me into the secret councils, you never listened to what I said—"

"We kept you from our secrets because you couldn't be trusted. We considered you unwise, Marco, we doubted your equanimity, your sense . . . And now we have proof of it. We saw pride in you, and knew you should never be trusted with power." Her measured words infuriated him.

"Indeed, we had severe doubts as to your suitability as guardian to Gerain." Miltus, one of the Geomancers, spoke equally coldly.

Gerain said, "Marco always did his best by me—" He was standing in the shadowy corner of the cave and it was clear that Marco had not realized he was there. He was looking very distressed, as if he had not slept for weeks.

"You!" Marco looked ready to knock Gerain to the floor. "What are you doing here?"

"Marco, I—"

"You cursed – traitor! You told them!"

"They had to know, Marco. It's too serious,

105

this, too dangerous! It's all going to go wrong!"

"I did everything for you!"

Zarah stepped between them. "Marco has been no friend to you, Gerain. Mixing you up in this wild scheme! So irresponsible!"

"You betrayed me!" Marco's eyes, fastened only on Gerain, were black as night. "You gave me away!"

"You said that the girls would never be allowed to leave! You implied worse than that!"

"I trusted you, you – fool! You could have been great, I would have made you my right-hand man—"

"Stop it!" Zarah held up her hand. "Enough of this. Gerain has shown only good sense. You have endangered all our lives, Marco. There will be reprisals. The Rustrians and the Soprafini will be after us now. Our only chance is to return the girls to the Rustrians—"

"And that will be difficult," said Miltus, slowly. "How can we return them without revealing how we live? They've seen it all. We may have to hold them after all."

"See? You'll do what I planned, in the end!" Marco was laughing wildly now.

There was a small silence as the Council looked at each other. Then Zarah said to Marco, "Your actions were foolish and reckless. We hereby decree that you are forbidden to practise the arts of aquemancy and geomancy. You will have nothing further to do with the prisoners. We will do our best to retrieve something from this situation, but you are to play no further part in this matter."

"I protest! If the arethusans are saved, this will be through my agency! You must know I acted only for the best!"

"Enough! Be quiet, Marco. Now, about these girls. . . ."

"Zarah." Gerain stepped forward. "The serving maid, the one called Philippa . . . She's one of us. There are scars between her fingers. We can't . . . just dispose of them."

The woman looked at him seriously for a moment. Her own hands were webbed. Then she glanced briefly to Miltus and the others for a moment's quiet consultation.

"I'll see for myself," she said. "An aquemancer without training could be dangerous."

"What do you mean?"

"If she goes back to Rustria, or Soprafini, they'll question her. And if she's got the power, if she can read water, then they'll use her. They'll use her to spy on us, they'll follow and find us. Remember, she owes her allegiance to *them*, to the Lady Maria, not to us."

"She's a servant, a slave—"

"Be quiet, Gerain. You understand nothing of

this. You two may leave us. We have important matters to discuss."

In the island castle of Rienzi, far away in the middle of the Bay of Stars, anger ran through the corridors.

"Call out the Guard." Ferdinand of Rustria rarely spoke loudly, even when he was really furious, as he was now. It was a conscious technique to keep people's attention, to keep them nervous and on edge. Ferdinand's soft voice cut like acid after his meeting with his secret council of pyromancers. "This is an affront to our honour. An insult which must and shall be avenged."

His son Ferrian was busy feeding baby birds to his red eagle. His large moist eyes were gleaming as he watched the claws pin the shivering chick while the hooked beak tore gobbets of red and white flesh. "We have to make an attempt to rescue Maria, I suppose. It would not do to appear weak."

Ferdinand laughed shortly. There was no humour in it. "Weak? This is a matter of *pride*. This time I'm going to smash the Barusi. This time there will be no escape to the mountains. I shall seek them, root them out, and destroy them!"

"And the Soprafini?" For once, Ferrian was

showing some interest in affairs of state. He was thinking of his pets, his fine Fireflies. They were getting hungry again.

Ferdinand shrugged. "The Soprafini will come next. If they think they can get away with foisting a spoilt, disloyal runaway on us, they've got another think coming!"

"So you don't want the girl back?"

"Do you?" His father's voice was even quieter.

"No. Not after this." The eagle was looking at him fixedly, waiting for the next course. Ferrian pulled another chick from his pocket and held it out. "Maria Soprafini deserves whatever she gets. I hope she rots, making me look stupid like that. She *jilted* me! Me, Ferrian of Rustria! I'd like to—" He stopped, watching the red eagle tear the chick to shreds. "She ran out. She's going to pay for it."

"It could have been a kidnap, of course."

"There was no sign of a struggle, no call for help. She'd packed clothes. She left *this* behind!" He held out the diamond engagement ring.

Ferdinand paused for a moment, thinking hard. Then he smiled. "No need to tell Gregor about it. We'll let the Soprafinians think that the marriage has gone ahead. It will keep them quiet while we prepare ourselves—"

"The Fireflies—" interposed Ferrian.

His father nodded, slowly. "Yes . . ." He looked at his son, at the cruel face of his only child. "I'll arrange it," he said. "Barusi first, and *then* Soprafini."

He looked at the map on the table in front of him.

"No more of this pathetic rubbish about treaties and agreements. I've had enough of it. The Soprafinians can learn a lesson from this, and I don't care who gets in the way." He scowled at his son. "It's a question of honour – your honour, my honour. It must not be said that the Rustrians were *lax*. The girl doesn't matter one jot. There's more at stake here. Do you understand?"

Ferrian understood all right. He licked his lips. "I'd like to get my hands on her, though. Just for a bit. . . ."

Ferdinand looked at his son with approval.

Gerain ran through the tunnels until he found a boat. Paddling hard, he came at last to the prison sector. Without hesitation, he turned down it, and reached to the place where the two girls waited.

He moored the boat, let down the bridge and ran across it. "Come on," he said urgently. "Come with me. I'm getting you out of here. You must come now."

Maria stared at him. "Why should we trust you?"

"Lady, don't argue. Go with him." Philippa, at Maria's side, had already efficiently bundled up the food in one of the cloaks.

"Just a minute." Another voice, Marco, this time. He stood at the other end of the wooden bridge, a knife unsheathed in his hand. "Just what do you think you're up to, Gerain?"

A hesitation, a fatal giveaway. "Zarah wants to see them. I was coming to get—"

"Don't bother lying to me." Marco kicked out with his foot at a lever. The bridge began to rise.

"Damn you!" Gerain leapt for it, his fingers just catching the edge of the wood. He dangled there, his feet only inches above the threshing minskies. They began to snap and jump at his heels, jagged rows of teeth gleaming in the unsteady light.

Marco leaned out over the water, smashing the heel of his dagger down towards Gerain's hands. There was a look of shock, of sheer and dreadful surprise on Gerain's face. And at the same time he swung himself forward and to one side, and his booted foot caught Marco in the gut.

He doubled over, the knife clattering to stone. Gerain swung himself again, making a jump at the end of the arc and finished up on the other side of the channel from the girls.

Marco was still incapacitated, but Philippa saw his hand move. "Gerain!" she shouted and at that moment Gerain threw himself to the side.

The knife fell harmlessly into the channel of minskies.

Marco was straightening up. Gerain caught him in a flying tackle and the two of them skidded over the rock until Gerain's head was almost dipping over the edge of the channel.

Maria screamed, and Philippa ran to the ledge where their provisions were. She picked up the water pitcher and without a second's thought, threw it at Marco.

It landed in the channel just beside Gerain's head. Water splashed up and into Marco's eyes.

For a moment he was blinded.

It was enough. Gerain rolled clear, falling on the lever which held the bridge up. Slowly, creakingly, it began to descend. The girls were across the bridge before it touched down.

And then a cry, a half-strangled moan from Gerain as he toppled over like a felled tree.

Marco stood there, breathing hard, the rock in his hand slightly reddened with Gerain's blood.

"Back over the bridge," he said, panting. "No more of this nonsense."

Philippa was on her knees by Gerain. "What

have you done to him!" she cried. "You've killed him!"

"What's it to you?" But his eyes flickered to the man at their feet, and he didn't see Philippa scoop up sand from the rock floor.

She flung it at him and he stumbled, his hands over his eyes, and Maria stuck out her foot and Marco tripped.

He fell, his right arm out to block the force of it, and his hand plunged into the channel of minskies.

A terrible scream as he rolled over, wrenching it out. There were two minskies clinging to it. He began to thrash his wrist against the rock, but Philippa and Maria were concentrating on pushing Gerain's inert body into the boat.

They could still hear Marco screaming as they paddled their way along the darkest, deepest tunnel of them all, not knowing where they were going.

CHAPTER 10

"Did you see it? Did you see his *hand*?" Maria covered her mouth with her fingers. "I think I'm going to be sick—"

"My lady, hush." Philippa was concentrating on paddling their little craft down the dark canal. There was a fork in the tunnel up ahead and she didn't know which way to go. She needed Gerain. She looked at the unconscious figure on the floor of the boat. "Can you . . . try to rouse him . . . We need help."

Maria leaned over the edge of the boat, her hands cupped together. She dashed water into Gerain's face and he stirred, groaning. Maria shook his shoulder. "Come on," she said,

114

"hurry up, we don't know which way to go."

Philippa felt a fleeting moment of sympathy as she watched Gerain struggle to sit up, his hand to his aching head. "What. . . ?" He blinked uncertainly at the blood on his fingers. "Oh, God. I remember." He looked up and ahead. "Turn round," he said. "They're both dead ends. We have to go back the other way, back to the market."

"They'll find us!"

"Not in those crowds . . . There really is no way through that way." He took one of the paddles and helped Philippa turn the boat. "But first we have to get past Marco. And his men." He looked desperate. "Where is he? What happened to Marco?"

"He slipped," Philippa said shortly. "His hand . . . went into the channel. The minskies . . . we didn't see anything else."

"God," Gerain said again. He was paper-white. They were coming up to the prison cave again. He stood up, somewhat unsteadily, and drew his knife from his belt.

At first the cave seemed deserted. Only a splattering of bright blood on the floor gave any clue that something had happened. And then they heard rather than saw a movement against the wall of rock to the right.

Marco was slumped there, his cloak wrapped

bloodily around his hand. On the floor beside him, two half-smashed minskies still twitched, their jaws snapping uselessly together.

He was almost unconscious. But as Gerain moved closer, Marco's eyes flicked open and his tongue moistened his lips. "You wait, Gerain. Just wait. You'll pay for this. . . ."

"Marco—!"

"You'll wish you'd never been born. . . ."

"I'll send someone for you. Hang on. . . ." Gerain got back into the boat.

Philippa frowned. "You're going to help him? How?"

"Just keep quiet." Gerain looked very grim. "You'll have to pretend to be my prisoners now. We'll never get past the tunnel entrance otherwise."

"But Marco?"

"I'll send one of the guards back for him."

"They'll know what you've done!" Philippa cried.

"He'll bleed to death if I don't." For a moment Gerain was quiet. Then he flung at her, over his shoulder, "I *have* to help him."

"For pity's sake! He tried to kill you!"

"He was doing his duty." And then the unforgivable thing. "He's the only family I've ever known. He brought me up. He's been like a father to me."

116

And then there was nothing more that Philippa could possibly say.

At the mouth of the tunnel, both she and Maria held their hands as if tied behind their backs. Gerain did all the talking.

"Zarah wants to see them, and now." He was already pulling away past the guards. "Oh, there was a bit of a struggle. Marco slipped, you'd better go and get him—"

"Why couldn't you have brought him with you?" one of the guards grumbled.

"In a hurry – can't stop."

And then they were through, and the market lay ahead.

It was as noisy and crowded and confused as Philippa remembered, but Gerain seemed to know his way around. They moved quickly, dodging here and there amidst the milling crowds, ever conscious that they might be followed.

Gerain was thin-lipped and frowning and neither of the girls could think what to say to him. They kept towards the centre of the lake, avoiding the cordons of dark-robed men who stood on guard at some of the tunnel entrances.

"They're on the look-out," he said at one stage. "You'd better keep down."

Beneath the heavy woollen blanket, Philippa craned her neck, looking for familiar landmarks. She realized, worrying, that Gerain was working his way across the market away from the area where they had originally entered the inland sea.

"Where are you taking us?" she whispered.

"The main exits are watched," he said. "There's a possibility . . ." he trailed off. They were approaching a chain of floating kiosks, lit by garishly coloured lamps. Women dressed in cheap, gaudy jewellery danced, half-naked men swallowed fiery daggers, musicians thumped and plucked and blew at a variety of unlikely instruments.

There were signs outside many of the kiosks, proclaiming wonders and lunacies. The boy with two heads, a bearded lady, the mermaid . . . Fortune-tellers promised accurate guidance from tea-cups, or palms, or the bumps of the head.

"Charlatans," sniffed Maria. "Cheap trickery."

"Don't knock it," said Gerain sharply. "This is going to be your passport to freedom, with any luck."

Maria stared at him, open mouthed. No one *ever* talked to her like that! He didn't even seem to notice the effect of his words, concentrating instead on positioning their boat alongside a tent of gaudy orange and white stripes.

A slightly grubby-looking girl sat at the entrance, filing her nails. She was wearing a greying kimono embroidered in yellow and scarlet. Her hair was black, falling to her shoulders in untidy clusters of curls. "Second show in half an hour," she said.

"Is Josquin there?" Gerain asked.

She said nothing, jerking her head towards the tent.

"Stay here," said Gerain to Philippa and Maria, tying the boat to a post. "I'll be as quick as I can."

Inside the tent the atmosphere was stuffy with smoke from an inefficient oil lamp. At first Gerain could see nothing. But then someone said, "Well, if it isn't Gerain Martel. And to what do I owe the honour of this unusual visit?"

A young man of medium height, with straight blond hair caught back in a knot, was sitting at a small table towards the back of the tent. A book of popular songs was propped up against a half-empty wine bottle. The remains of a meal lay scattered on the stained cloth. He was dressed in severe black, with frothing white cloth at the throat and wrists. Ruby pins, stuck into the foaming lace, glinted in the light from the smoking lamp.

The rubies were made of paste, Gerain knew. It was all part of the act.

"Josquin, I need your help."

"I've got a show in thirty minutes. It had better be quick."

"I want to get away from here. Without being seen. Marco will be looking for me—"

"Wow, what did you do? Disrespect towards your elders and betters?" The blond man's eyes were laughing.

"Worse. Much worse." Gerain paused. "It's no joke, Josquin . . . I don't know what else to do."

"You'd better sit down. Tell your Uncle Josquin all about it." He still sounded amused.

"You don't understand. This is serious."

A slight pause as Josquin considered him. "As it happens, this is our last show for the Barusi. It's the jolly old road to Soprafini after this. I expect we could squeeze you in somewhere. You'll have to join the act, of course. Your voice wasn't bad, from what I can remember—"

"There's something else." Gerain had reddened. "I'm not alone. I've got two friends with me—"

"Dear me, whatever possessed you? Our virtuous young hero, so dedicated, so—" Josquin was being frivolous but then he stopped, taking in the expression on his friend's face, the smear of dried blood on his forehead. "And what will the 'friends' contribute to the travelling road-show? Do they sing too? Of course, we can always do with some strong arms to shift scenery. . . ."

Gerain shook his head. "They're women," he said. "And one of them's a princess."

Another, much longer silence. "And I'm a Rustrian riddler," Josquin said softly at last. "Just what have you got yourself into, my old friend?"

For answer, Gerain left the tent, and returned a moment later with the two girls. "This is the Princess Maria of Soprafini, affianced bride to Ferrian of Rustria. And her serving maid, Philippa. . . ."

Josquin stood very still, his eyes running over the two women. "No." He sounded very definite. "No way. I'm not getting mixed up in this, princess or no." He bowed, gracefully. "My regrets, ladies. We don't take passengers."

"Josquin, they're not going to be allowed to leave here. They were kidnapped—"

"By whom?" Josquin's eyes narrowed.

Gerain hesitated. "Me, I suppose. It was Marco's idea. Marco planned it, but I actually got them out of Rienzi."

"Don't tell me, you climbed the walls? I *knew* it would get you into trouble one day."

Gerain shrugged unhappily. "Marco said that if we held Maria hostage, they'd have to unblock the Ere. That *we* could force the issue and save the arethusans."

A soundless whistle from Josquin. "Dreams of grandeur, Gerain. Marco must be off his head, meddling with Rustrians and Soprafinis. How on earth did you get mixed up in this?"

Gerain said nothing, uncomfortably regarding his hands.

"Don't tell me, the great hero promised honour and glory. You were always so *idealistic*, Gerain. So trusting. How long did it take you to see the light?"

"When I realized that Marco wasn't going to let them go again. He was going to keep them prisoner or—" He stopped.

"Or what?" Philippa sounded very cold. "Kill us?"

"Why do you think I betrayed him?" Gerain shouted. "I couldn't let him murder you!"

"You betrayed Marco?" Josquin asked.

"Yes. I told the Council what we'd done."

"Well, surely you're all right then. I don't see what all the fuss is about. They'll help the ladies on their way—"

"No!" Gerain groaned, running his hands through his hair. "They've seen everything here. They'll never be trusted. Zarah won't let them go . . ." Gerain looked at his friend. "There's no easy way out of this, Josquin. I didn't want to involve you, but they'll all be out looking for us now."

He broke off as a bell rang, not far away, sounding clear and strong over the water.

"Fugitives!" yelled a man's voice in the distance. "People of Barusi, beware. Loose in our land are spies from Rustria, two women who could reveal all our secrets to our enemies. They must be apprehended at all costs, living or dead. A great reward, three bags of gold, will be offered for their return."

Further away, they heard another bell, another man shouting the same message. And then the news was passed from place to place throughout the inland sea, until every kiosk, every boat and ferry and barge must have heard it. It echoed everywhere.

Josquin sat down, slowly, at the small table. He steepled his fingers together. For a while he said nothing. "You're asking not only me, but all the troupe to risk their lives," he said bleakly. "Gerain, *think*!"

Gerain said, "Marco almost killed me just now." It was difficult for him to say the words. *My friend almost killed me. I betrayed him and he almost killed me.* It repeated in his mind like some evil incantation. "I think . . . he must be mad," he said with some difficulty. "He wants to overturn the Council. He wants to rule Barusi.

We have to get Maria out of this, away from here. It's going to be dreadful here."

Maria cleared her throat. "I promise a reward of thirty bags of gold, if you help us."

Josquin stared at her, unblinking. "Really? Well, that would be nice." He clearly didn't believe a word she said. "I'll have to ask the others. I'll try. But don't bank on a result. I can't do anything until after the show. Can you keep out of the way for a while? I'll be back later."

He stood up, nodded to the girls, and left the tent.

Maria sat in the chair he had just vacated. "Well, what a rude young man. He won't help us, anyway. He's much too concerned about his own skin."

Gerain looked distracted. "It might work. Josquin owes me one. I stopped his boat from going over the Drop once. We were best friends when we were children."

"Won't Marco look for you here? If you've always been friends?" asked Philippa.

"He never approved of the theatre. I used to meet Jos secretly. It was ages ago, anyway. I used to skip classes and stay out late. . . ."

"It must be good to have a friend like that," said Philippa.

"Don't you have anyone, back in Soprafini?"

"I'm a slave. Slaves don't have friends," she said shortly.

"What about you?" he asked Maria.

Maria looked at Philippa. "Only Pip," she said, slowly, as if it was some kind of revelation. "Princesses don't have friends, either. There were courtiers . . . but they were so concerned with their own advancement, their position. It was very formal, at home. And Lassan, I wonder now if perhaps he was the same. He didn't try to stop my parents sending me to Rustria, he just waved goodbye. There's never been anyone else."

Gerain made an effort. "Well, I suppose you've got me now, too."

"It's got to be an improvement. You did get us out of that cave, I suppose." She coloured faintly and put out her hand to him. "Thank you, Gerain. If – when – we get back to Soprafini, you will have every honour."

But Philippa, who had been staring into the handful of water she had scooped up from the lake outside, said nothing. She didn't think Maria was going to be bestowing those kind of rewards ever again.

CHAPTER 11

They waited in the tent while Josquin sang love duets with the girl outside. They were all nervous. Gerain kept twitching the tent-flaps, trying to see if they had been found out.

The performance seemed to go on forever. It took place on a proper stage, set with curtains and wings and gas-lights. The stage had been erected on the wide barge moored next to their own. The stage itself was tiny, a miracle of delicate and ornate woodwork, gilded and painted, and only when she looked very carefully did Philippa notice that the whole thing was hinged. Probably it could be collapsed and packed away and carted off to the next booking in a matter of minutes. How ingenious, she thought, how very clever. . . .

The girl had changed out of her tatty clothes into a tight-fitting sequinned top and a skirt made of feathers. Her hair was piled high on her head, one raven lock falling to the shoulder. From a distance, she'd probably look just fine, Philippa thought.

"They're rather good," she said, with some surprise.

Maria was not so generous. "Vulgar. And she sings flat. It's a cheap show, badly presented." Maria prided herself on her own singing, Philippa knew. She had had the very best teachers, after all. It wasn't just snobbery.

Still. "I think you're a bit unfair. Josquin sounds all right." She wondered how she dared contradict Maria like this. Without doubt, the balance of their relationship had changed.

For a moment it looked as if Maria was going to lose her temper. Philippa turned away from her mistress and sat down at the table opposite Gerain. "They won't take us," she said. "They'd be mad to risk it. Perhaps we should slip away now, before someone turns us in."

He sighed. "I don't – honestly – think we have any chance of getting away without Miracule's troupe. All the exits and entrances will be rigidly policed. It's never easy, getting out of Barusi. Remember what it took to get in here."

Philippa knew what he meant: the waterfall, the rapids, the arethusans. . . .

Gerain was still speaking. "I think our only chance, really the only possibility will be to travel with the Players. Of all people here, they are the only ones with a legitimate reason to leave. And they've always been known as a mixed bunch with odd hangers-on. They've been calling here every autumn ever since I can remember. We'd be fitting in with a recognized routine."

Maria said, "They'd be fools to risk it."

Philippa looked at her mistress in surprise. This was a degree of realism which she did not normally associate with Maria Soprafini.

"We have no alternative." Gerain looked at her seriously. "I . . . can only apologize. I never meant it to come to this."

"Well, what good is that?" Maria spoke acidly. "It's done now."

"But you didn't want to marry Ferrian, did you, my lady?" Philippa said, greatly daring.

"No. Anything – almost anything would be better than that." Their eyes met. Both girls were thinking the same, remembering that pit where the Fireflies raged.

There was a spattering of applause from outside as the brief show drew to a close. But instead of returning to the tent, they heard Josquin cross over to the next kiosk. Over the distance they heard raised voices.

"He's called a meeting," Gerain said. "Cross your fingers, say your prayers. Whatever seems appropriate."

It didn't take long. All too soon, Josquin pulled back the tent opening. There were two people behind him, a thin elderly man dressed in the blue robe of an aquemancer, and a large woman with silvery hair and a floor-length costume embroidered with blue-grey sequins that looked like fish scales.

Josquin was trying to bar someone from the tent. Philippa caught a glimpse of raven curls, heard the girl's voice upraised with anger. Firmly, Josquin drew the tent opening together and shook his head, as soon as he saw Gerain.

"Princess – Your Highness – may I introduce my uncle, Miracule Miracalia? He is in charge of our little troupe. And this is the Lady Aqurelt."

The two elderly people bowed to Maria. Josquin said, as if glad to get the formalities over, "But it's no good. I'm sorry, Ger. We can't risk it."

"My regrets, Your Highness. They've doubled the guard at the exits," the older man said. Thin eyebrows almost met over his nose. His eyes were kind, his skin deeply wrinkled. "Everyone leaving is searched, every item of their baggage gone through. You'll never make it, and we will find ourselves in great trouble, to no good purpose. I'm sure you understand our position. You may be best advised to give yourselves up."

"They'll be killed!" Gerain repeated.

"I think not. They'd never dare, not if this really is the Princess Maria. My apologies, Your Highness." His hands lifted, palms upwards. "I can see no alternative."

At his side the Lady Aqurelt hesitated. She whispered something in the man's ear. Miracule looked more closely at Philippa. "Young lady," he said. "Where do you come from?"

"I was born in the mountains," she said. "Taken to Soprafini after one of the raids."

"She could be one of our own," said the woman, longingly. "She has the look of it, those green eyes. . . ."

Miracule's eyes were full of compassion as he looked at his wife. "Now, my dear. It does no good to worry over such things, there is nothing we can do, not on our own. You must put that out of your mind."

Neither of the girls knew what he was talking about.

"I can sing," said Maria, hardily, returning to

the point. "We could work for our passage, and they might not notice . . . Can't we join your troupe?"

"We already have singers enough," said Josquin's uncle. "And magicians and dancers and fire-eaters—"

"I can sew and dress-make," said Philippa, reluctantly. "I could help with costumes."

"You're used to working, anyone can see that." He took her hand and turned it over, tracing the scars between her fingers. Miracule shook his head. "But it makes no difference. We cannot chance this."

Gerain drew himself up. "I thank you for your patience. I trust the rest of the tour goes well—"

The woman's face softened. "You're a good boy, Gerain. I wish you well." And then Miracule Miracalia and the Lady Aqurelt bowed low to Maria and left the tent, leaving Josquin behind with the fugitives.

"I'm sorry," he said again. "But what did you expect?"

"Did you talk about it to the whole company?" Gerain asked.

"No." Josquin shook his head. "Not everyone can be trusted . . . three bags of gold is a considerable bribe to impoverished entertainers. It didn't seem fair to put them under that burden. Only Miracule, Aqurelt and Sylvie know—"

"Sylvie?"

"My partner. My singing partner."

The girl with raven hair, who had tried to join them in the discussion. . . .

"Well, what now?" Maria looked at Gerain as if he should hold the answers.

"Hide, I suppose. Try to lose ourselves in this lot."

Together they moved out of the tent and looked around the vast cavern, the thronging crowds of people and boats. Another act was taking place on the stage, and the crowds were gathering to watch a red-haired woman tie herself into unlikely knots to the accompaniment of some feverish drumming. There was no sign of Sylvie.

"Everyone will be looking for us." Gerain gazed out over the heads of the audience. "Keep your eyes open for men in brown particularly. They're Marco's followers. Council people are generally dressed in blue. Don't talk to anyone."

"If I may make a suggestion?" Josquin said. "Disguise yourselves. Dye your hair, change your clothes. I can help you with that, at least."

It was good sense. He led the way to another tent and started to rummage through a chest full of oddments of clothes.

Velvets, satins and net fell at their feet. "Aha,"

said Josquin in triumph, holding out a flimsy pale green skirt to Maria.

"I can't wear that!" She was outraged. "It's not at all respectable. People will see my legs!"

"If they're looking at your legs, they won't notice your face," said Josquin, smiling at her dismay. "And what a pleasure they'll be missing!"

"I've got a better idea." Philippa didn't approve of this familiarity. "They're looking for two women and one man. What if we both dress as men?"

"Now *that* is inventive." Josquin sat back on his heels, regarding the two girls. "You'll have to cut your hair."

"No!" Maria didn't stop to think. "I've never cut it! I can't—"

Her hair fell in long, blonde tresses she could sit on, if she wanted to. She was extraordinarily proud of it. The court poets at Soprafini had held competitions in honour of it. She couldn't bear. . . .

Philippa was holding scissors.

Maria swallowed. "I suppose I can always grow it again."

"Atta girl," said Josquin. "Now, how about these breeches?"

Two hours later, four young men took a boat across to one of the refreshment kiosks. They all drank beer, but the two smaller lads weren't all that enthusiastic. They ate roast chicken and new-baked bread, but anyone watching with a careful eye would have seen that those same two smaller boys weren't at all handy with their fingers. They seemed to find the grease unpleasant, and looked ill-at-ease amongst the noisy rabble.

Beneath the hastily-applied wash of grime, Maria was rather pale. "I keep thinking someone's *looking* at us," she whispered to Philippa.

"Just relax." Josquin had heard her. "You're doing fine." But Philippa noticed his eyes ceaselessly scanning the crowds, running from face to face. She swallowed another mouthful of beer and wondered if she would ever understand why people liked the stuff.

"So, what will you do now?" Josquin asked.

Gerain put down his pint mug. "Lie low, I think. We don't have much choice. Sooner or later the fuss will die down." He forced a smile at the girls. "Cheer up, it could be worse. You could be still in that cave surrounded by minskies."

"Don't remind me." Philippa was looking at the crowds. "How many people live underground here?" she asked.

"No one's ever counted. I don't know . . . fifteen, twenty thousand perhaps? All this range is a warren of tunnels, most of which are filled with water. And there are plenty of people, not only the Barusi, who prefer freedom to rule by the Rustrians or the Soprafini—"

"My father is a fair and just ruler!" Maria raised her chin, a challenge in her eyes.

"I don't doubt it for a moment, Your Highness." He spoke quietly. "But not everyone wants to spend their lives in pursuit of the fine arts."

"Humanity's highest accomplishment!"

"Maybe. All I'm saying is that there's more than one way to sing a song, more than one dance to tread. They're a mixed bunch, here. And I certainly prefer the Soprafini version of life to that of the Rustrians any day. All that military training, that rigid discipline."

Maria unbent a little. "It was . . . something of a shock," she agreed. "I had no idea what it would be like. My parents didn't really tell me much—"

"They didn't *tell* you much? About where you were going to spend the rest of your life? Didn't they *care*?"

"They wanted the treaty to go through." She stared straight ahead. "What I felt didn't come into it."

"They didn't even go with her Highness to Rienzi," said Philippa unwisely. She thought

135

later that it must have been the effects of the beer. "They weren't even going to attend the wedding—"

"You are speaking out of turn, Philippa. I must remind you that it is not your place to criticize—"

"I've got a suggestion," said Josquin, breaking in. "Just until you get back to Soprafini, why don't we forget all about titles and treaties and rewards and court life? You're three fugitives, you have to stick together, and matters of protocol are just going to get in the way. What do you think, Princess?"

There was a long pause while Maria considered it, her mouth entirely unsmiling. But before she could speak, before she could dismiss this outrageous idea with a few well-chosen words, Gerain suddenly reached out and caught her wrist. "Look!" he hissed. "Over there—" And just across the water from them, at a distance of only a hundred yards, a barge full of brown-robed men was approaching.

In the stern sat a man with a very white face, his hand wrapped round in blood-stained bandages.

Marco.

CHAPTER 12

"Quickly!" Josquin seized Maria's hand, pulling her back into the crowds round the bar. Gerain and Philippa were not far behind. They ducked together under the counter, keeping low as they ran the length of the serving area, between the skirts of the waitresses.

There were a few screams, and someone stuck out a foot and sent Gerain sprawling, but no one made any kind of serious attempt to stop them.

There was a door at the end of the counter, leading through to the kitchens. They ran, knocking a tray from someone's hand and sticky, greasy soup splashed all round them.

There was more serious opposition in the kitchen but Josquin lashed out and Philippa head-butted the enormous, aproned stomach of the chef as he blocked the back door. A clatter of copper pots and pans crashed around them.

Then they were out amongst the rubbish bins and jumping across the small channels. They were seen, but another chaotic and messy plunge through a coffee kitchen threw the men in brown off the scent.

At last, breathing heavily, they fell into the bows of an ancient barge. Josquin pulled up the canvas covering and they crawled beneath its shelter. For a moment no one said anything, concentrating on getting their breath back. There was a strong smell of chicken soup.

"That was your friend Marco!" said Josquin bitterly, at last. "He's found us!"

"It's aquemancy. He's one of the best," Gerain said.

"Well, are they always going to find you?" Josquin sounded pessimistic. "How are you ever going to get away?"

"Something's giving us away." Gerain was puzzled. "Someone."

"What about your theatrical friends?" asked Philippa, diffidently. She didn't want to offend anyone. "Do you know them all well? Might one of them—?"

Maria took it up. "What about that girl, what's-her-name, Sylvie? She didn't look very friendly."

Josquin shook his head. "No, she wouldn't do anything like that, not Syl. I'm sure she wouldn't—" His voice faded.

They fell into a depressed silence.

"Are there really no unwatched exits?" Philippa asked at last. "This place is a warren, how can they control it all?"

Gerain sighed. "They sealed off all the smaller tunnels during the tribute raids. It was a matter of defence. I mean, when I was little there were hundreds of ways to the outside. Many families had their own exit."

"How were they sealed off?" asked Philippa.

"Most of them were flooded. Others were filled with rubble. It's no use, Philippa, we won't make it."

"Gerain, what about the water chute?" Josquin said suddenly. "Was that closed up, too?"

"It was blocked off after that little girl was lost. Too dangerous, they said . . ." Gerain sounded thoughtful.

"Water chute? What's that?" asked Philippa.

"When we were children and there were more arethusans around, some of us used it as a playground . . . It's a series of interconnected waterfalls and lakes which lead to the plain on the south side. We used to hang on to an arethusan and slide down it as a treat. And then the arethusan would tow us back up to the top. It was a great feeling . . . but one day a child drowned, partly because the arethusans were weakening I think, and they refused to do it again. The priests say that the girl's spirit is trapped under the water there, that the route is cursed. . . ."

"Do you believe that?" asked Josquin, curiously.

"I don't know . . . No. Not really. It's a horrible place now, but we could give it a try, perhaps. . . ."

"I'm tired," announced Maria. "Let's talk about it later. I need to sleep."

"Of course, my lady," said Philippa through the force of long habit.

Josquin disagreed. "I'm sorry, Your Highness – um, Maria, but you really cannot afford to stop now. This entire area will be searched."

"What do you mean 'you'? If there's even a chance that your friend Sylvie *did* give us away, you'll have to come with us. I think you're part of this now, whether you like it or not," said Maria. In the dim light beneath the tarpaulin they saw Josquin's face change.

The wide grin had completely disappeared.

"I couldn't go back, anyway," he said savagely. Beneath the conventional good looks, they saw that he was passionately concerned. "It might put Miracule and the Lady Aqurelt at risk. I couldn't bear to get them into trouble."

"They're your family?" Maria asked.

Josquin shrugged. "Sort of. It's a long story, I'll tell you about them some other time. If we ever get out of here. Let's concentrate on that. Miracule and the Lady will understand, they always do. So, the water chute?"

"We'd better have a look at it. Just check it out," said Gerain, leading the way.

They almost didn't make it. There were watchful men with knives in their hands everywhere, men who asked questions all the time. Some of them Gerain recognized, and knew that they were Marco's followers. Others were Council men, and their knives were no less sharp.

Somewhere along the way, Josquin "borrowed" a small skiff which was coming adrift from its mooring. "Well, if people can't tie their boats up properly, what can they expect?" he said when Maria complained that she was not in the habit of associating with thieves. He seemed more amused than upset by Maria's disapproval.

This was the only element of humour in the escape. The chute lay on the far side of the cavern, over a mile distant. The quickest way would certainly be across the centre of the lake, but this was terribly exposed.

Gerain suggested they cut across the west side of the cavern, where the wrecks and unused boats were moored. It was a lonely area, largely unlit. They could get out into the centre from there, no one would see them.

It was a long way, and there were too many people everywhere. But the little stolen boat helped, dodging in and out of the crowds. Both Josquin and Gerain were adept at handling it, and Philippa soon picked it up. No one suggested that Maria give it a try.

She sat in the prow of the boat, her face averted from them. She looked as if she was in the grip of some terrible dream, something that she couldn't quite believe. She sighed audibly and shifted uncomfortably on the wooden seat.

The others paid her no attention at all. There was nothing they could do, after all. Their progress was slow. It seemed for ages that they only ever doubled back on themselves, or as if they were going in circles. But gradually Philippa realized that they were, slowly and painfully, making their way to a less populated area of the lake.

They had plenty of scares, like when Maria suddenly panicked and nearly fell out of the boat because she thought she'd seen Marco. She hadn't, but the commotion attracted too much attention.

And then, when they had nearly reached the deserted jetties, they suddenly heard someone shout out Gerain's name, loud and clear.

"Gerain! What are you doing over here? This isn't your usual patch!"

Disaster. There were three Council men standing a little way beyond the friend. Gerain stood up immediately, blocking the view of Josquin and the girls seated just behind him. The boat rocked wildly. "Hi, Perry . . . Just a moment!" He stepped out of the boat, hissing under his breath, "Go on! I'll lead them off. See you at the chute. . . ."

As they pushed away, towards the shadowy areas, they could all see that the Council men were watching Gerain. One of them suddenly frowned and spoke hurriedly to his companions. He brought out a whistle and blew it, and all three men started running.

Gerain was off, leaping from boat to boat, making very fast for the rock wall at the edge of the lake.

Philippa, Maria and Josquin watched his zig-zag, tense with anxiety. The Council men paid them no attention; their boat was too low in the water to be seen.

"What will he do?" asked Philippa. "How will he lose them?"

Gerain had reached the edge of the lake. He stood at the bottom of the rock-face for a moment, estimating his chances. The pursuers were not far behind.

Philippa saw him jump, like a cat, for a hand-hold. For a second he swung there from one arm. And then he began to climb, quickly and efficiently. They could just make out his lanky form, spread out against the rock-face like a starfish. All around him, the rock was broken by tunnels and caves.

"He knows the rock backwards. He'll have some plan," said Josquin confidently, although the look on his face did not match his voice.

There was a great deal of activity now at that side of the cavern. There were Council people pushing through from all sides. In all the fuss, the little boat with its three remaining passengers managed to slip away, out to the cold dark centre of the lake.

"Which way now?" said Maria.

The lights and crowds were far behind them. The dark shapes of abandoned boats and barges bobbed silently all around them. There was no sound apart from the faint slapping of water against empty hulls.

Josquin was scanning the rock walls, his eyes creased up with strain. "God, I don't know! It's years since we played with the chute. I was only a child, I really can't remember."

They paddled between the wrecks. Broken masts jutted overhead. "What we really need is an aquemancer," said Josquin. "Oh, for a pair of webbed hands—"

"Do all aquemancers have webbed hands?" asked Philippa quietly.

"The best ones do." He was still scanning the distant sides of the cavern. "Why?"

Philippa hid her hands. "I just wondered," she said.

This was all deeply disturbing to her, throwing up ideas she hardly dared admit. Was she really a Barusi aquemancer? Would she find people who knew her here? Might she still have a family somewhere? These thoughts were turning her world inside out, but there was so little opportunity to come to terms with them. They were on the run, pursued by people who wanted to shut them up forever. . . .

She only knew that she didn't understand who or what she was.

Black arts. Aquemancy and the other magical skills were called black arts in Soprafini. They were associated with evil-doers, with perversion and secrecy. But gazing at water was irresistible to her. She'd always been so lonely, so lost at the Court of Soprafini. Maria was her closest companion, but never forgot that Philippa was a servant. There was no equality in their relationship.

It had been a comfort, somehow, to have a secret that no one else shared, an unknown strength. To reveal it now would be to diminish it.

"What does the entrance look like?" she asked Josquin.

"You can't see it directly from the lake," he said. "It's hidden away up the side of a narrow creek."

"Well, why don't we just move along the side of the rock wall?" she suggested, sensibly enough. "We're bound to come across it sooner or later."

Josquin turned the boat without hesitation. In silence they threaded their way through the blackened hulks to the wall.

Slowly they inched along it. There were any number of openings in the rock-face, but Josquin shook his head. They fell into silence, worrying variously about the future, about Gerain, about aquemancy. It seemed like days had passed before they found the narrow creek, but it could only have been a couple of hours.

The creek cut straight into the rock wall, no

more than three metres across at its widest point. A little way along it an ancient barge had been crammed between two outcrops of rock.

"There," breathed Josquin, with relief. "Behind that."

Over the top of the barge they could just see another tunnel winding through the rock. With some difficulty they clambered over the wreck, hauling up the stolen skiff after them.

Behind the barge a low tunnel ran deep into the rock.

"What about Gerain?" said Philippa, when they were all in the boat on the other side.

"We'll wait," said Josquin. "I think we're safe enough here for a while. Let's give him a chance."

In that dark and empty tunnel, they huddled together.

They knew they wouldn't sleep. They were too cold, worried and uncomfortable. But when, some hours later, Maria shifted against Philippa's arm and opened her eyes for a moment, she gave a muffled scream to see the dark swathed figure climbing into the prow of their little boat.

"It's all right," said Gerain. "It's only me."

They were all awake then, exclaiming with relief. Even Maria seemed glad to see him.

"However did you do it?" said Josquin as they set off down the tunnel. "I thought they were bound to catch you—"

"Well, you know how I climb. And I remembered this part of the cavern from when we were children. It wasn't generally known, was it? Don't you remember that the arethusans themselves showed us how the chute worked? It was like a secret between them and the children. I don't know that there were any adults in on it."

They paddled on. The tunnel varied in size, with shiny black walls and high, arched ceilings in places. It seemed to have been made for different craft, boats that might have had masts and sails, like the wrecks they had seen in the great lake. But no one sailed here now; no breath of wind moved the surface of the oily black waters.

Philippa shivered. Gerain was telling them about his childhood, how the water chute had worked, but his voice echoed strangely in the dark. He didn't mention Marco once, although they all knew that Gerain must be thinking of him. He trailed to a stop, and then nothing was heard apart from the soft swish of their paddles.

At one point the tunnel opened into a wide cavern and there was a noisy rush of flapping wings as a colony of bats took off, skimming around their heads. Maria shrieked with fright.

"They won't hurt you," said Josquin calmly.

"My hair!" she cried. "They'll get into my hair!"

"No, they won't, it's far too short. They never get in people's hair anyway, they're very clever. . . ."

And sure enough, the pointed, leathery wings came nowhere near. But the nearly inaudible squeals had unsettled them all, and they were cross and touchy with each other.

Beyond the cavern the tunnel narrowed. The paddles kept knocking against the wall, so in the end they just guided the boat along, pushing their hands against the slimy rock surface. Maria just watched.

"It never seemed as narrow as this, when we were children," Gerain said, puzzled.

"Did you come by boat?" asked Philippa.

"No. I suppose that's it . . . The arethusans found us in the big cave. This was really the start of the ride."

The tunnel wound through a series of bends until, without warning they suddenly came up against a blank wall of rock, reaching down into the water in front of them.

"What's this?" Josquin said.

"It was never here when I was a child. I don't see how—" Gerain was disturbed.

"Perhaps the water level has risen," said Philippa. "There may be a way through, underneath. . . ."

Gerain nodded. "That makes sense."

She ran her hand over the rock. It was clammy with damp. "Do you remember how it went here? Was there an arch? Didn't you have to duck down, as children?"

He smiled at her. "I'm glad one of us has got some common sense. Yes, you're quite right. The ceiling was low for some distance . . . twenty metres perhaps. We could probably hold our breaths and make a swim for it—"

"What?" Maria was appalled. "You cannot be serious!"

"Lady, believe me. It's perfectly possible, I assure you. I remember how it goes."

"No we can't," Philippa said. "The Princess Maria can't swim. Neither can I."

"No problem." Josquin's wide grin gleamed in the dull light. "A rope round the middle and we'll pull you through—"

"Did you bring a rope?" said Gerain.

"Isn't there one here? In the boat?"

But the boat was small and ill-equipped. "Couldn't we tie our cloaks together?" Philippa suggested.

Gerain shook his head. "Not strong enough . . . If you'll trust us, ladies, Josquin and I could take you through. If you'd allow it?"

Philippa shook her head. "It would make you too slow. What if your estimate is wrong? It was a long time ago. What if it's more than twenty metres? You two, unencumbered, could probably do it, I'll give you that. But *not* towing someone else."

They stared at each other.

From far away, far down the tunnel, they felt a disturbance in the air. Something lifted the hair from their scalps, caused their hands to clench. They all remembered the story of the child who had died.

A faint sound, a sigh and a ripple on the water which suddenly rocked their little boat, rocked it from side to side as something passed by. . . .

"Arethusans!" breathed Philippa.

Gerain was on his feet. "No!" he shouted incredulously. "It can't be, they never come down here now, they never come—"

But looking over the edge of the boat they saw the sinuous shape, the silvery fur, the clouded emerald eye of an arethusan gleaming at them.

"Hey!" Josquin had thrown his hat into the air. "He's even wearing a harness, you'll be quite safe, ladies. . . ."

"You mean – you mean we have to go *under-water*?" Maria was not in the least reassured.

"Unless you can think of some other way to get through twenty metres of solid rock." Gerain shrugged.

"I think it's the only way, Your Highness—" began Philippa, but Maria interrupted.

"No. Absolutely not. There must be some other way—"

"There is not. You'll be quite safe—" said Gerain.

"No, we'll have to find some other way. You cannot possibly expect me to do this kind of thing. This is simply not on."

"There is no other way," repeated Gerain slowly, as if to a child.

For a moment it looked like she was going to hit him. She turned from one to the other of them, looking for support. They all looked back at her. No one said anything.

A long pause. And then Maria swallowed. "I'll wait here, then. You go on. I'll – go back, give myself up . . ." Her voice faded to a halt.

"You just have to concentrate on holding on. And don't breathe out. . . ."

"I can't!"

Looking at her, Philippa recognized deep-seated panic. This was not just Maria being the spoilt princess. She was genuinely terrified. "I'll go first," she said. "I'll send the arethusan back with this—" she pulled her green silk handkerchief from her pocket, "to show that I made it safely."

"No!" Maria clutched her arm. "Don't go, please don't leave me—"

"Lady . . ." Philippa looked into her eyes. She didn't like doing this, it went against all her life's training. "Lady, there is *no* choice. There is *no* other way." She saw Gerain taking off his boots and bundling them into a cloak. She paused. "I don't want to force it—"

"Force? What are you talking about?" Maria drew herself away, her eyes wide and panicky.

"I'll go." And without another word, Gerain took a deep breath and dived into the black water.

The arethusan whisked along beside him and after a terrible interval – was it three minutes? four? – came back with Philippa's handkerchief attached to its harness.

"There, see?" Josquin held out the dripping rag to her. "You'll be all right."

"I just – can't . . ." Maria's hands were still shaking.

"Now listen to me." Josquin's voice was light and calm. "Lady Maria, look at me." And he struck a match, lighting a taper. The light gleamed in his face, and she stared at the wide-spaced blue eyes, the calm mouth and straight nose. He was really unfairly good looking.

"Maria, do you want to live? Think about it. We're doing our best to help you, to get you out of this mess. You have to forget about being special, about what's due to you. You could try helping us, for a start. You'll feel better if you're no longer a victim. It's better to act, to take part. Believe me."

Maria spoke through gritted teeth. "I just can't! I can't do this, I'd rather—"

"Trust me," was all he said. He held the light before her face and moved it gently from side to side. And then his voice began to repeat, softly and monotonously, "You will be quite safe. You will take a deep breath, and hold on and you will be quite safe. There is no need to fear. Take a deep breath, and hold on. You will be safe."

After a moment's stunned incomprehension, Philippa realized what he was doing. She moved quickly, guiding Maria's unresisting hands to the strap of leather trailing from the arethusan's harness. She twisted the leather round the princess's wrists.

"Hold on," she whispered. "Lady, hold on." Josquin had taken off Maria's shoes, had taken the cloak from her shoulders.

"I'll go with her," he said. "To make sure. . . ."

Philippa nodded. Together they helped Maria over the side.

"A deep breath, my lady. A very deep breath – now!"

And the arethusan flexed its back and plunged down, and Josquin threw himself into the water at the same time.

The last thing Philippa saw was Maria's white, heart-shaped face, blank and dreamy. The wait went on forever. And then the arethusan re-emerged alongside the boat and shortly after it, Gerain, red-faced and spluttering.

"She's fine," he said quickly. "Furious, but fine." He looked at the boat, which contained everyone's shoes and boots and outer clothes. "I came to help with the boat and luggage," he said, tying it all securely together. "And to reassure you . . ." He suddenly grinned and took Philippa's hands. He looked totally different, much younger, much more approachable. "It's all right. I really think we're going to make it, I really think we'll be all right!"

"Thank you," she said calmly. "There's still a long way to go, surely?" And she wound her wrists in the leather strap, took a deep breath and slipped over the side.

CHAPTER 13

It was an avalanche of a ride to the outer world. The arethusan was joined by another, and the little boat surged along the narrow tunnels and across empty lakes, towed by the two silvery creatures as if their lives depended on it.

The journey was often interrupted. Gerain said that the terrain had changed, that there must have been rockfalls and floods, because he no longer recognized where they were going. The route they were now on was dangerous, complicated by submerged rocks and sudden changes of level.

In the past, when Gerain and Josquin had

taken the chute, they had been out in the sunshine within an hour. This was taking much
longer. The route was often precipitous, the
water rushing and crashing down the steeper
gradients. At those points, they left the
arethusans to jump and shimmer over the rapids
and hauled the boat out of the water. With great
difficulty, they manoeuvred it down slippery
slopes of rock and shingle. It was surprisingly
heavy out of water.

They were all soaked to the skin, shivering all
the time. It was so cold. Their teeth chattered,
their hands shook. Philippa wondered grimly if
they would ever feel warm and dry again. That
wasn't all. There were many minor injuries.
Everyone was covered with cuts and bruises
from slipping on the rocks. And sometimes
there was just no way to climb down the rapids.
They had to trust the arethusans to guide the
boat safely through and it capsized several
times. None of them were in serious danger,
because the arethusans always managed to be
in the right place at the right time. But sooner or
later, Philippa thought, one of us is going to get
badly hurt, and then we'll really be in trouble.

But she had to admit things could be worse.
At least Maria wasn't playing up. Their two
companions did their best to shield her from
the worst of the clambering, but she pushed

them away. Her mouth set, her face pale, she kept going without complaint. Josquin's words seemed to have had a considerable effect.

It was Josquin who suggested they pause after about an hour of half-drowned battering. They were slumped on a slippery fall of rock to one side of the main channel. They were all shivering constantly, catching their breath with difficulty. The boat had just turned tail for the third time, and Philippa had struck her knee painfully against a submerged rock. She rubbed it vigorously, wondering how the others were making out. There was the narrowest chink of light from somewhere up ahead, and she could see a pale gleam from the others' faces.

She noticed that Josquin looked only at Maria. Well, she was likely to be the weak link, thought Philippa. Life at court was no preparation for this kind of thing.

Philippa cleared her throat. "I'd rather keep going," she said through teeth that chattered sharply around the words. "We won't get warm here."

And this was true. Everything was soaked.

"Maria?" Josquin looked at her. "Are you ready to move on?"

She nodded briefly, her face turned away.

Philippa touched her arm. "Lady, are you all right?"

"Let's go." She pushed away Philippa's hand and scrambled back into the boat.

Philippa watched her lean forward and stare into the icy water. She sat there silently, watching the slight movements of the arethusans below.

Just beside Philippa, Gerain said, "Is she often like this?"

Philippa shook her head. "She's changing. I've never seen her so – quiet – before. I tell you one thing, though. She's managing better than I thought. She really is." She sighed. "Come on. We'll all feel much better when we're dry."

And so they got back into the boat and at last made it out into the sunshine.

Broad daylight was temporarily blinding. They were in the foothills of the mountains and the river they had just been towed through glinted and sparkled in the sunlight.

It was not noticeably much warmer. Although the sky was a clear and brilliant blue, there was a fresh breeze disturbing the leaves on the trees.

"All the better for drying," said Josquin optimistically through teeth that rattled together. "Cloaks first . . . and then we can all be perfectly decent while everything else dries."

They threw the sodden cloaks over bushes that were already beginning to turn yellow with the approach of autumn. Philippa wandered around gathering the small, crimson berries growing there. They were on the sharp side, but better than nothing. They were all ravenous.

Gerain had disappeared into the woods with his knife at the ready, announcing that he was going to find something proper to eat. "I don't much fancy nuts and berries. A nice plump rabbit or two, that would be the thing. . . ."

Josquin was left with the job of trying to make a fire. He soon found some flinty stones at the side of the river. There were plenty of dry twigs scattering the hillside. A certain amount of cursing, and many increasingly impatient attempts before a small flame flickered beneath his fingers. He crouched low, blowing gently at it, coaxing it to life.

Maria watched him listlessly. She sat on a rock by the river contributing very little. Between blowing sessions, Josquin kept up a flood of chatter, telling her about his life with Miracule and the rest of the troupe.

"My own parents had a singing act. Mum sang, Dad played the lute . . . They died when I was very small, three years old. I don't really remember much about them. There was a bad outbreak of 'flu that year. Half the troupe got it, and not many of them recovered. . . .

"Miracule brought me up as if I were his own

son. He's my dad's brother . . . The Lady Aqurelt joined him two years later. They've always been together since then."

"They're married?"

He grinned. "I don't know. Something like that. Funniest step-parents anyone ever had. A magician and a mermaid. You should have heard the bedtime stories. Aqurelt's frame of reference is – something else. The bogeyman was always an octopus." He smiled at the recollection.

"So didn't you go to school?"

"We were on the road." He shrugged. "How could I? The Caccini brothers taught me maths. They're both drummers, counting comes naturally to them . . . Miracule made sure I learned not only to read, but how to remember. I can quote you anything you like. He's an actor, of course, as well as a magician. And Ruby taught dancing and singing, and Finkle showed me how to cook, and Timor taught fencing and the high wire. Nature study and geography sort of happened naturally, because we were always travelling. We've been everywhere. I can sell you tickets to the show in nine different languages. The complete education, don't you think?"

"Perhaps . . ." She still sounded bored.

He looked at her, considering. "Tell me about your life, Maria."

She shook her head.

"Come on, I really want to know. It's not every day I get to speak to a real princess—"

"Very well then." Her voice was cold and hard. "I had tutors for everything, the best in the world. Professors and instructors and academics. I did physical sciences, languages, history – at *huge* length – everything. The Archbishop himself taught me scripture. The great artist Uccelini showed me how to paint flowers. I had the best of everything."

"Well, that must have been quite something."

"But it was no *use*! No use at all! I can't . . . climb walls, or perform on stage, or hunt rabbits or anything! You had to *hypnotize* me, I was such a coward . . . I feel so stupid, Josquin. You were quite right. I don't contribute anything of any value."

"But Maria, none of this is your fault. You can't help the education and upbringing you received. No one can. You shouldn't feel bad about it—"

"I would have loved to learn cooking and weight-lifting and how to swim—" she cried and then stopped. A small grin, a first glimpse of self-mockery. "Do you think it's too late?"

He smiled at her. "Anyone can learn anything. If they want to."

"Go on about your life. I love hearing about

it." She seemed a little happier so he turned back to the fire.

"The best thing about my weird education was that I finished up with a whole bunch of foster-parents. I never knew who was going to put me to bed. A whole family of adults paying me attention. They're great, all of them. . . ."

"What about Sylvie?"

"She was a late addition to the clan. A mixed up kid with nowhere else to go . . ." He sighed. "We had – something going, but it was very vague."

"But now you've left her behind," she said bleakly. "You've left them all behind. Risked everything, to get me out."

"You, and Gerain and Philippa." He sat back on his heels, looking at her. "What now, Maria? Where do we go from here?"

"To Soprafini, of course."

"Your turn again. Fill in the gaps. What about your marriage? This treaty with Rustria?"

There was a long pause. Then she said, "The marriage is off. Even if they took me back after this, I cannot possibly marry Ferrian. I never wanted to, but it seemed . . . It was considered a political necessity." Her voice dropped. "The trouble is, I think it was all misjudged."

"What do you mean?"

"Well, when we were staying in Rienzi, we

were shown all round. They have barracks for thousands of soldiers, soldiers with weapons I'd never even dreamed of! Their workshops are incredible. There are vats of stinking poison, explosive missiles that could be sent hundreds of metres! I didn't understand any of it, how any of it worked." She shook her head unhappily. "It's all so efficient and it must be in order to *do* something. You don't keep weapons like that in a state of readiness if you don't expect to use them. And the Fireflies – need fuel. Need people to burn up and destroy."

"Fireflies? My God. They really exist? And Ferrian's in charge?" Josquin looked very shocked.

"He was so pleased with it all, so proud. I hate him." She stared at the small fire crackling on the ground beneath Josquin's hands. "At first I was impressed by the look of it all, by Ferrian's style. He dressed in cloth of gold! The jewels. But there's something so cold about his horrible, fishy eyes. And you can see his mind weighing you up, calculating your usefulness, your worth . . ." She shuddered. "And he's cruel. He likes to watch things suffering, animals and people. . . ."

"What has this to do with Soprafini?"

"More food for the Fireflies. It's what really worries me."

"You think the Rustrians really are going to attack Soprafini? Whether you marry Ferrian or not?"

It was a relief that he understood so quickly.

"I don't think the marriage was of the least significance, not to the Rustrians. It was all a bluff, a diversion to lull us into some idea of security. I think the Rustrians are planning to take over the whole of Maquerlia with the army and the Fireflies. I don't know how anyone could defend themselves against the Rustrians, especially now that the Fireflies can be transported."

"And your parents had no idea of the Rustrians' intentions? They were prepared to marry you off without really knowing the situation?" He sounded incredulous.

"It's different, being a princess," she said, with difficulty. "I'm not – a private person. It was always understood that I would have to marry to benefit Soprafini. When Lassan—" She stopped.

"Who is Lassan?"

"Oh, someone I used to know . . ." She looked very unhappy.

He felt an urge to put his arm round her shoulders. Instead, he put some more dead wood on the fire, carefully building a small pyramid of twigs.

"Lassan was one of the courtiers. He came of good family, but it wasn't enough . . . He was a wonderful poet, really talented."

"Did he write poems about you?"

"Sometimes." And then a tear overspilled from her eye and ran down her cheek. "It's not fair," she said. "I had to say goodbye to him, and go to Rustria . . . that's why we were so relieved when Gerain came to get us out. I thought he came from Lassan, I thought he was one of Lassan's men."

"You soon discovered your mistake, then."

"Yes . . . you see, the only reason for me to return to Soprafini is Lassan. I don't want to go home, my parents will think I failed. I've really let them down. They'll just send me back to Rustria, to that useless marriage anyway. They'll do anything to appease the Rustrians. This — escape – is a godsend. But you'll still get your reward," she said, and saw him frown. She hurried on. "You don't have to worry. Lassan's family is very wealthy . . . when his father dies, he will be Earl of Luria."

"I didn't do this because of the reward." He stood up, away from her. "Perhaps your education didn't prepare you for that. Gerain is my friend. You don't buy friendship with bags of gold."

She was appalled at her mistake. "I didn't

mean – I'm sorry. That was offensive."

He studied her unhappy face and thought, It's not her fault. All those posh tutors and instructors, and she knows nothing, less than a baby.

Poor little princess.

He dragged the conversation round again. "So if you marry Lassan, you'll be a countess?"

"Well, why not?"

"It's a step down from Queen of Rustria or Empress of all Maquerlia." He turned back to the fire, not looking at her.

"I don't care about that. What does it matter, anyway?"

"Well, what about this Rustrian army, then? Won't they use your escape as an excuse to attack?"

She shuddered. "Yes, they may very well." Her tone was very flat. "Whatever I do, either I or everyone else will be miserable. I can't see any way of making things come right."

"There's the arethusans." Gerain had come up behind them, two fat rabbits in his hands. "If you saved them, then you'd know you'd done something right. Without question."

Maria paused. Like Philippa, she had been both fascinated and puzzled by these alien aquatic creatures. There was something so eloquent about the expression in their faces, something so – human. And not human.

"But how can we help them? They need their breeding ground again and the river's dammed. The treaty doesn't mention the dam at all. No one in Rustria or Soprafini thinks it's at all important."

"But you are. You're important, Maria. Perhaps you could tell the world what's happening, make them notice. . . ."

"It's not like that. They'll take no notice of me. They never do." And because neither Josquin nor Gerain had any idea what court life was like, they let it rest there.

That night, full of casseroled rabbit and berries, they wrapped themselves in their warm, dry cloaks and curled up round the fire. But no one slept, not for a long time.

CHAPTER 14

Maria thought: Oh, what have I done? I can't go home, I've let them all down. The treaty has been broken and there will probably be war . . . I can't go back to Rustria and marry that awful Ferrian, absolutely not. They probably won't have me now, after this. And the Barusi, those mountain people: they just want to use me, and anyway we injured that man Marco, they're our enemies too. I have no friends, no one to trust. I like them, I like Josquin and Gerain, but it's no good. I always say the wrong thing, I'm no use at this kind of life. I'm hopeless. I don't know what to do.

On the other side of the fire from her, Josquin

lay on his back, watching the stars. Maria loves someone else, he thought – this poetry-spouting Lassan of good family . . . damn him! And anyway, why should she look at me, a third-rate singer now out of a job, on the run, with no prospects, no connections. She's a princess, for God's sake! She's used to fine clothes, the best food, wonderful houses. What do I know about etiquette, about water-colours? But her hair, that fine blonde hair . . . and those eyes, deeper blue than any I've ever seen, almost violet, amazing. She looks good dressed as a boy, she's slim, long legs . . . She'll never look at me, our lives are too different.

Gerain was closest to the river. He lay with one hand dangling over the side, almost touching the surface of the water. The arethusans went deep at night, far away from the river bank. He thought of them longingly.

And what hope for you, my beautiful ones? Can we get your river to run again, when none of the powerful people are in the least interested? When foolish alliances come first, before your wonderful grace, your magical power?

He had not told the girls why the arethusans were so important to the Barusi. They knew nothing of the great choice: indeed, no one had been able to make the choice in Gerain's memory, because of the dam, blocking the river. The connections between the Barusi and the arethusans went deeper than outsiders ever understood. Even Josquin had no idea of the real relationship.

Thoughts of the Barusi were not comfortable for Gerain. He had betrayed Marco, hoping to make things better, hoping to get the girls released, but it hadn't helped. He knew that Marco would never trust him again, but he had hoped for some sympathy from the Council. But now that he'd run away with the girls, they wouldn't trust him either. He would never be able to return.

And Philippa looked from one to the other of her companions and made a fair estimate of all their thoughts. She knew they were all unhappy in their various ways, and that there was not much she could do, here and now, to cheer anyone up.

Better think what to do next. She didn't want to return to Soprafini, the home of her slavery, where her skill was so mistrusted. And with all her heart she loathed the Rustrians, with their violent, rigid, soulless society. They needed a war, she thought with horror. Imagine, to *want* to destroy, to fight and maim . . . They needed new territories, new populations to plunder for the Fireflies. Maria's disappearance would give them a pretext to attack. They would claim that Soprafini was behind it . . . She shivered, although she was no longer cold.

And the Barusi were out for their blood. The Barusi, who were probably her own people . . . She'd never find out who she was now. They were surrounded by enemies and impossibilities. She needed some clue, some pointer to the future. For a while she lay there, fighting the impulse. And then she rolled over and listened carefully. From the sound of breathing she decided that those nearest to her, Maria and Josquin, were asleep. Carefully, she stood up and crept away from the dying fire towards the river.

Below her, somewhere in the depths, the arethusans swam. Did they sleep there, she wondered? What dreams ran through their dark, drifting underwater life?

She was filled with yearning. More than anything she wanted to know about them.

On a rock at the edge she bent over and cupped her hands together. Webbed fingers would indeed do this better, she thought, disturbed. The arethusans have webbed hands and live in water all the time. Perhaps they understand about visions, perhaps they lived with visions all the time. Their life beneath water was somewhere totally beyond her imagining.

She sighed, peering into the water between her hands. It reflected only stars back at her, and she tried to calm her thoughts.

No wind to ruffle the surface now, no heavy drops of rain. It was very quiet. Around her she knew the stillness of the ancient hills waited, that a thousand rivers murmured, running from the plateau far above them.

She could see none of this. She looked only at the dark circle of water held in her hands and repeated under her breath the meaningless syllables of a watery mantra, something she had found useful in the past for clearing the mind.

Black, cool water, cupped in the bowl of her hands.

She leaned further forward and saw her face reflected back at her . . . but was it her face?

And again, that feeling of loneliness. Two wide eyes, a small snub nose, a baby mouth . . . the face of a small child, a baby, stared at her.

"Who are you?" Philippa breathed.

Tears welled into the wide eyes, spilling over the plump cheeks. The child was too little to talk, but to Philippa the message was clear. This child was lonely, abandoned. *Go away, I don't need you.* The words suddenly formed between them. *Go away, I want* . . . The child was choking on sobs, desperate, lost in sadness.

"Who are you?" asked Philippa again. She

was terribly moved by the child's anguish. But the face was withdrawing, disappearing, fading into blackness, and all she could see was that lake again, that wide stretch of dark water rolling back, under the shadow of a webbed hand, revealing something she couldn't see.

She felt such sadness from this poor abandoned child, that she could hardly concentrate on the dark water in her hands.

She blinked her own tears away and when she looked again, the constellations of stars overhead gleamed back at her. The Leaping Fish, the Pestle and Mortar, the Queen's Sabre shone at her . . . She had never seen them so clearly in water before. But their patterns were subtly altered: they looked like the shape of bones, white bones reflecting like a hand, a hand again, through the water, pointing at her.

A hand of bone, pointing to her face, to her eyes.

With absolute terror she stumbled backwards, throwing the water far from her.

"What were you doing?" Gerain, standing just beside her. She'd had no idea he was there. "That was aquemancy!"

"What? No, it's not, I never learned magic—"

"Maybe not, but I've seen magicians concentrate on water like that a thousand times. Philippa, what did you see?"

"Nothing. Nothing was clear, it doesn't always work—"

"I don't believe you. Why are you so upset?"

"It's not allowed, I could get into trouble—"

"More trouble than we're in already? Would that be possible?"

A pause. In the starlight she found his face kind and concerned. He wasn't angry with her, he wasn't mocking anything . . . He was Barusi, and used to aquemancy.

"I wanted to see where we should go next," she said in a small voice.

"And what did you see?"

"A lake. Set in mountains, a deep, wide lake . . ." She could not speak about that sad child, she could not share that with anyone. It wasn't her secret anyway: the child wanted someone else. "And the water rolled back in great waves, and there were bones there, white bones gleaming, like a hand pointing to us—" She was shaking again and felt nothing but gratitude when he put his arm round her shoulders. "It was Marco!" she said. "It was his hand, pointing to me—"

"He's tracking us. It has to be that." Gerain looked bleak. "It's because we're travelling over water. He can find us like that and he won't give up, not Marco. Tell me about this lake. What shape is it?"

Her own hands were still wet. In the starlight she traced an oval on the rock in front of them, an oval with a bulge to one side.

"There are mountains around it," she said. "And a great river runs into the lake, coming from the north . . . I think I recognized it, but I'm not sure." She looked at him. "Do you know it?"

He groaned. "I know *of* it," he said. "It's the lake formed by the damming of the Ere."

She remembered then that journey from Caer Corelli to Rienzi. They'd crossed the dam then, but it had been night. She'd not been able to see anything. "Where the arethusans are blocked from the sea?"

He nodded.

"Can't the arethusans breed there, in the lake?"

"They need sea water. And they hate that lake. They never go there." He paused. "They behave as if it's cursed or something—"

She stared at him. "Do you believe in curses, then?"

"No . . . we saw no signs of that drowned child in the tunnels, did we?"

She shook her head. She could say nothing. Not in the tunnel, no. But here, under the stars, a child had called to her.

Gerain was still speaking. "But still . . . I

believe in aquemancy. I've seen it work too often."

"When? Tell me about it." She wanted to know everything about aquemancy. She needed to know that it wasn't just an accident or an illusion that she could see visions in the water.

Gerain said, "We used aquemancy to find you in Rienzi. It's how we got you out. Water reflects, you see . . . Marco could use it to see into places far away. He probably *is* tracking us now . . . He could look into a bowl of water and focus it on any place he wanted to, if there's water there . . . He saw Maria and you in Rienzi because the whole place is surrounded by water. He could even tell when the patrols took place. It's a very useful skill, Philippa, if you can do it too."

"So aquemancers *do* see what happens to real people then?"

"Oh yes . . . If they're good, and know what they're doing . . . And some of them can see into the future."

She thought about the lake. "What I see isn't happening now. That lake . . . is full of water at the moment, isn't it? No one's drained it yet."

"No." He looked at her seriously. "It's important to the alliance, Maria says. It proves that the Soprafinians trust the Rustrians. It's the bridge between the two countries. But that doesn't matter now. The arethusans do. They're more important than two squabbling neighbours."

"You haven't seen the Rustrians. You haven't seen Fireflies in action. Honestly Gerain, they're completely terrifying."

"I accept that. But think of what your vision has shown you. Perhaps it's telling us what we should do. Perhaps we really should find some way of getting the arethusans through to the sea."

The river at their side was suddenly disturbed as the two arethusans surfaced and for a moment two pairs of vivid green eyes gleamed before they disappeared again into the water.

"Breach the dam, do you mean?" She stared at him with excitement. "How *could* we?"

"Aquemancers are powerful people, Philippa. Especially when it's combined with a touch of geomancy—"

"What? Who's a geomancer?" She looked startled.

"You are, Philippa. You're a climber, a natural mover over stone. It's always the first sign. It often goes with aquemancy, anyway. Marco's an aquemancer although he hasn't got webbed hands. The only touch of magic I've got is a bit of geomancy. That's why I can climb as I do. You've got a touch of both. Who knows what you might be able to accomplish?"

The idea astounded her, its implications were shattering. She thought back over her childhood. Yes, there had always been that fascination with water, and she had known that to be something special. But the skill at climbing she had just taken for granted. She had always managed to find herself some remote part of Corelli to stare into water, and it had often entailed her climbing out of windows, scaling the walls to the deserted roof.

She knew that other people could not climb as she did: she thought it was just her good fortune. But it was only a small skill, something of trivial usefulness. How could it possibly help to breach a dam? These ideas were too big, too momentous.

And then there was that little child in her vision. That was private. She couldn't tell Gerain about that little weeping face, the child who hadn't wanted Philippa. She knew that the child was a secret, something that must remain hidden and protected, sending a private message – but not to Philippa.

They settled down back by the fire and Philippa knew that she wouldn't be able to sleep, not after all that. But as soon as her head touched the bundle of bracken they were using as pillows, she fell into a deep, dreamless oblivion.

*　　*　　*

In the morning, Gerain tried to explain about breaching the dam. Strangely, the most objections came from Josquin.

"It's wild," he said. "Madness. Some half-baked vision . . . with all due respect, Philippa, you say you've never trained in aquemancy."

"I know," she said humbly. "But it's never been inaccurate before. And have you any better suggestions?"

That stopped him dead. They were lost, all four of them. In exile, out on their own, with no safe haven, no community of friends.

"The terrain's very hard. There are the marshes, those reed meadows . . . And mountains again, serious mountains. The river's not easy, there are rapids, gorges . . . And we're in autumn now, and winter's not far behind. . . ."

And indeed they had all noticed the chill in the air that morning, that sharp clarity in the sunlight that might in a day or two turn to frost.

Josquin was used to travelling. He knew what he was talking about. More than any of them, he knew what it was really like to live on the outside.

"We've been to Lake Ere," he said. "We did an autumn tour once, round all the farms which were getting the harvest in . . . It's really wild there, there's hardly anyone there."

"You'll know the way then," Maria said.

"Maria, you do understand what Gerain is suggesting? He's planning to breach the dam, to destroy the route from Rustria to Soprafini. I don't know how he's going to do this, it'll be heavily guarded," Josquin said.

"It's a brilliant idea." They all stared at her. "It'll delay them. Keep the Fireflies out. Come on, think! We've got to do this, it's the only way to make things right!" Maria looked at Josquin, her eyes bright and glittering. "You'll show us the way, won't you?"

And although he had been about to protest, to say again that it was impossible, lunatic, he shut up. Because Maria expected him to help.

He sighed, picking up his cloak and draping it over his shoulders.

"Right then," he said. "We'll need other provisions if we're going to make it to Lake Ere. We'd better put together some kind of an act."

"A stage show? Like gypsies?" Philippa looked nervous.

"Well, I don't see why not." He turned to Maria. "Have you any marketable talents, Princess?"

"I can sing," she said coldly. "Better than you. And play the lute."

"Do you know this one?" He began to sing a folk song, a simple melody familiar to them all.

Maria calmly folded her hands together and cleared her throat. Her voice was pure and true, singing an elaborate descant to his line.

At the end of the song she slightly inclined her head, as if waiting for the applause.

Gerain and Philippa clapped, as required. But Josquin folded his arms. "Not quite the right style for that song, don't you think? A bit over-ornate—"

"What? How dare you criticize—"

"I'm a professional!"

"The Court of Soprafini cheered my performances!"

"Well, they would, wouldn't they?"

"Stop it!" Gerain was disgusted with them. "It's not a competition. You can both sing, you can work something out without getting at each other. . . ."

"And what are you going to do?" Maria said acidly. "Climb walls?"

He flushed. "I'll find the food, go hunting, make camp. . . ."

"And what about Philippa?" Maria turned her brittle attention to her maidservant. "What will you do?"

"Oh there's no problem there." Gerain answered for her. "Philippa's an aquemancer. She can tell fortunes."

Maria pursed her lips. She was still flushed

with anger. "Fortune-tellers! Crooks, all of them. Magic!" She spoke with loathing.

"It's not magic!" Philippa said passionately. "I just found that – sometimes I could see the future. If I looked into water, sometimes, just sometimes, there would be pictures there."

"Theatrical fortune-tellers don't usually bother with magic anyway," Josquin said mildly. "It's not at all essential to the job. They just watch their clients carefully. People give things away without meaning to. And they all want the same kind of things, riches, health, a lover . . . Anyone can do it." He took hold of Philippa's hand and gazed deep into her eyes. "Lady, you have experienced sorrow and loneliness (this one always works, because it's true for everyone) . . . but a turning point is at hand. A stranger will enter your life, someone with a message you should heed—" He let her hand fall, not noticing the blankness in her expression. "See?" he said. "It's easy. Any old waffle will do, so long as you're sure to include a tall dark stranger (or a beautiful blonde, depending on the age and sex of your client)."

"I couldn't do that." Philippa was indignant. "It's leading people on with lies."

"Not at all. All you're doing is giving them a bit of hope, a reason to go on. It's a kindness, really."

She still looked doubtful.

"I think we should be moving," said Gerain. "We can discuss this on the way. But we need to put space between us and the Rustrians. And the Barusi."

For a moment all of them looked up at the mountains they had left behind, at the cascading waterfalls and rivers that tumbled from the lake at the top. Something flashed; caught in the sunlight far away. Gerain shaded his eyes and squinted. "Men in uniform," he said. "Uniforms . . . Blue and white colours. And something else . . . *cages*?"

"Rustrians," said Maria in a small voice. "With the Fireflies."

"They're already trying to get inside the mountain," said Gerain. "They'll be looking for you—"

"There's nothing you can do to help the Barusi now," said Josquin. "They'll soon find out that the princess has gone."

"Then they'll be after us," said Maria. She picked up her cloak and put it on. "Right. Let's be off."

And with the arethusans whisking through the river beside them, they started down the long track to Lake Ere.

CHAPTER 15

The Rustrians were moving fast. They scoured the upper plateau, combing through each cave, sending men down the potholes following each streamlet and river until it either dropped over the edge or disappeared into the ground.

"They're down there somewhere. It's just a matter of time." Ferrian's thin rat-face was confident. He was staring at the roaring cataracts pouring over the edge of the plateau. Almost unconsciously, he adjusted the jewelled gauntlets on his wrist. "It's a nuisance, that's all. We should have obliterated the Barusi years ago."

A man in captain's insignia rode up to the prince. "All honour, Highness."

"Your report?"

"Sire, one of the divers has been found drowned."

"Where?"

The captain pointed towards the great river, where the worst of the rapids frothed.

"Careless. . . ."

"Sire, there was a bruise on the back of his neck. Of course there are many rocks there, and the river runs fast. . . ."

"But you think this no accident?"

The captain hesitated. "No. It was not an accident."

Ferrian's leather-clad fingers drummed against the pommel of his saddle. "Very well." He signed to one of the sergeants to come forward. "You have the poison ready?"

"Yes, sire." Behind them stood a wagon filled with wooden barrels.

"Half of them into the great river, then. Spread the others between the tributaries." He watched as his soldiers rolled the barrels off the wagon towards their various destinations, a smile of satisfaction on his thin lips. Blank, fishy eyes followed the yellow staining of the clear water. "Well, my Barusian friends. You sought to cross me, did you? See how you like this token of my feeling for you. . . ."

He raised his voice over the rush of water. "Over the other side of the plateau. Get the Fireflies into position. They may try to escape out that side, I estimate." He pointed to the south. "If there's anyone left. . . ."

The raw stump of his arm burned like acid. Marco's eyes flitted around the faces of the Council of Aquemancers. Less than half a dozen were there. The rest were all dispersed throughout the inner sea, trying to soften the effects of the poisoned water.

Sulphurous gas soured the air. In the few hours which had passed since the barrels had been emptied into the river, fumes from the poison had spread everywhere within the mountains, carried by the rushing waters. Poisoned gas penetrated along all the tunnels, through all the caves, widely over the inner sea. Nowhere was safe. Several members of the Council had covered their noses and mouths with scarves.

"Let me go after them!" he said.

Zarah spoke impatiently. "For goodness' sake, Marco! There's more than enough to do here, without wasting time and energy on that band of young hotheads—"

"I'll bring them back!"

"No, let them go. What happened to your hand was a great tragedy, but not murder." She had to stop for a moment, assailed by uncontrollable coughing. "Not like adding poison to the river," she said at last, her eyes streaming. "We have more urgent things to consider."

The lights over the lake were subdued, the noise had died away. There were no hawkers yelling their wares now, no brightly lit kiosks offering exotic entertainments. The boats were all stationary, apart from the dark-shrouded barges which collected the afflicted. People were talking in hushed whispers, some were crying. Most people had covered their mouths and noses against the stench, but the sound of coughing rang everywhere.

A sickly yellow fog hung over the surface of the water. It smelled of sweet almonds and bad eggs, and choked in the throat.

At the edge of the cave where the Council habitually met, the arethusans were leaving. They were disappearing, a ripple of silver in the water, down a dark, unlit tunnel. Marco watched them go with utter fury. They had been his route to power. If he'd managed to save them, he could have named his price. The Barusi would all have regarded him as a saviour, a messiah. . . .

It had all failed because of that wretched Maria

Soprafini. Because of his traitorous ward.

Further round the sea he could hear the moaning and vomiting from those who had swallowed the water before realizing that it was poisoned. Some twenty, mainly the elderly and young children, had already died. There would be more before long.

"It was a wild plan, Marco. Madness! How you and your ridiculous followers could ever think of bringing us all into such danger by kidnapping Maria Soprafini, I cannot imagine. And now look what we have to cope with. . . ."

"There is still no fresh coming through?" Marco snapped at one of the men who had just come towards them.

The man shook his head. His boots and breeches were all stained yellow by the liquid. He was exhausted and dispirited. "It's still running cloudy. They must have great tanks of the stuff!"

Zarah looked dismayed. "It'll get through to the river towns. There will be massive loss of life. All the fish, all the animals which drink from streams and rivers. God help them all!" She turned to Marco. "If you must do something, go and help the volunteers at the upper levels. There must be some way of diverting the stream—"

"What use am I with this?" Marco was shouting

now, brandishing his bandaged forearm at her. "Listen to me! We need to get them back. Then we can bargain with the Rustrians. I bet they've got an antidote somewhere . . . We need to bring those fools back to face what they've done!"

She spoke again, sternly. "Marco, they are irrelevant now."

"Not to me. I'd lose my other hand and both feet too, to have five minutes alone with those little hussies and that cursed traitor."

There was an appalled silence. "You are ill, Marco. Feverish. You do not know what you say."

"I know exactly what I say. You none of you understand what's going to happen. As you know, all our troubles revolve around the existence of that ridiculous princess and her farcical marriage treaty. A permanent alliance between the Soprafinians and Rustrians will be the end for us. We *have* to get her back. Then we can bargain—"

"For heaven's sake, Marco, put this idea of bargaining out of your mind! Sooner bargain with a rattlesnake than with the Rustrians!"

He stared at her in fury. Then he turned his back on her and walked away.

Bargains. Marco understood very well how they worked. You offered something – a skill, a hostage, a bribe, and bought something else you needed. Well, he had no hostages now, and unless he was very careful, his great plan to save the arethusans and so take over the Barusi was nothing more than a dream.

He was pacing the cave where he and Gerain had lived. He'd never forgive Gerain. That this boy, this child he had guided and trained and influenced, should behave like that!

Gerain was going to pay, no two ways about it. But first, Marco had to get the fugitives back. That was the priority, the central thing. Once he had them in his power, he'd be able to call the tune, with both Barusi and Rustrians . . . But there was no one to help him. His followers had dispersed, caught up in the emergency.

And then he paused in mid-stride. Perhaps there was another way. Perhaps he could still make it work. His own people had turned against him: they were no use to him. Forbidding him to practise aquemancy! If the Barusi weren't prepared to believe him, to trust him, he'd have to look elsewhere . . . And the Rustrians would be looking for the runaways too.

Perhaps they might be glad of some help. Perhaps a Barusi aquemancer might have something to offer them, even if he was minus a hand.

The Rustrians were the most powerful force Maquerlia had ever known. Why should he waste time with a people who spent their lives in hiding, who were incapable even of defending themselves?

Perhaps he might find the power he craved in the hands of the Rustrians.

That night, as Marco climbed slowly up through the upper tunnels towards the Rustrian encampment, a party of travelling entertainers, led by Miracule and the Lady Aqurelt, found their way out of the mountain by a different exit. They had followed one of the Barusi's own secret passages, one that lead far underground over to the forests to the east of the mountains. They were going to travel south, because that was what they often did in Autumn. Aqurelt and Miracule were in perfect agreement. They would go south towards Soprafini, and perhaps, just perhaps. . . .

The pyromancers who'd accompanied Ferrian to the mountains were baffled. They'd even tried to use aquemancy, but Rustrians were temperamentally unsuited to water magic. Marco would have sneered, if he'd dared, at the ornate golden bowls suspended from creaking tripods. Heavy, gilded mirrors stood all around the golden bowls, reflecting the starlight at the water. It was all an elaborate waste of time, as far as Marco was concerned.

The Rustrians achieved results with these means. The trouble was, they were wrong.

And Marco, drifting in and out of fever, saw only nightmare visions, pointing with a skeleton claw hand through the shadowy water towards his former ward and ally, Gerain.

"They've left Barusi, and they're making for Lake Ere," he said, his voice curiously uneven. "And there is a connection, there is someone using the watery screen, an aquemancer of some power with them—"

"Another of your people beside Gerain?" Tracho, Ferrian's chief adviser and master of the Rustrian pyromancers, frowned.

"It's the maid. Philippa. She's at least half Barusi, we estimate. And she's the one looking into the future, not us—"

"A clairvoyant?" Tracho looked stunned. "A true far-seer? Who *is* she?"

Ferrian thumped his fist on the table. "Where are they? How far? That's what matters. Enough of this mystic rubbish!"

"It's not clear—"

Infuriated, Ferrian motioned the Rustrian pryomancer forward. Chanting pious words, Tracho poured water from a silver jug and swirled it around beneath the open night sky.

He held out his hands and allowed his acolytes to take his cloak. He took a deep breath and leaned forward over the bowl.

Over his shoulder, Ferrian could see nothing in the dark water but the vague glimmer of stars.

"To the west," said the Rustrian. "They travel to the west and you should send your armies that way—"

Marco shook his head. He tried to keep the contempt from his voice. "You're wrong. They're going south, towards Ere. Think, where else would they go?"

"And have you indeed come to help us find these fugitives?" Ferrian said. "Or are you trying to throw us off the scent?"

Marco hauled himself to his feet. He was light-headed with loss of blood, distracted both by pain and by the uneasy suspicion that there was still a hand attached to his left forearm, that its fingers moved and indicated what he wanted to know.

"I want them back more than you do," he said. "I want to crush and destroy the man who did this—" He thrust the bloody bandaged stump at Ferrian. "And you have made me a promise. Remember? You have promised me acolytes to train, a position at Court as

Aquemancer to Your Royal Highness – you have promised me time alone with the man who betrayed me."

"Indeed, that is what I have promised." Ferrian shrugged.

"It's what I want more than anything in the world!" Marco shouted.

"All right, all right. You cannot want your traitorous friend back more than I want to get my hands on Maria Soprafini. You just point the way, and we'll get going."

"They've gone south. Believe me. Your pyromancers know nothing."

Ferrian stared at him for a long time. He was used to weighing men and usually found them wanting. In Marco, he found an arrogance and a passion that he could use. And an exceptional skill, one virtually unknown in Rustria. So Ferrian stepped forward, his arm outstretched.

"I think you are a man I can deal with. I think that, for once, a Barusi and a Rustrian might work together for mutual advantage." He nodded for one of the slaves to help Marco into a chair, and for food and wine to be brought.

"Now," he said. "How far south do they travel?"

CHAPTER 16

Josquin's Jollification gave their first show at a farmstead three days later. It was a party to celebrate the last harvest of the season, and people had come from far around. Long trestle tables were laden with roast meats, bowls of spicy rice, dishes of vegetables and fruits and cakes.

There were barrels of beer and wine lined up against the barn wall and by the time the Jollification started up, everyone was well away.

It was perhaps fortunate. Josquin was of course a complete professional, and did a series of comic monologues, ranging from a Soprafinian dandy to a moaning mother-in-law.

He was totally convincing in each role, his whole body reflecting age, class, health . . . He could be anyone, Maria realized. As flexible and versatile as a chameleon.

But the rest of the show was a little ragged round the edges, to say the least. They did their best, and all Gerain received for his juggling was a squashed tomato, and a rival group of singers started up when Maria sang her solo. The tune was the same, but the words very different. . . .

She was disgusted. Maria considered that her performance was worthy of serious attention. Everyone had always listened in respectful silence in Soprafini. . . .

"What did you expect?" Gerain was short with her. He had resented that tomato. He'd been doing his best . . . And his ideas about mutual respect had dwindled away during the three days on the road from Barusi. "They don't know you're anything special. They've heard a hundred singers before, and besides they're here to have a fine old rowdy time. You should think yourself lucky that you can pass yourself off as a boy. It would be a thousand times more difficult else."

Philippa had been reluctant to tell fortunes. For the first performance, she just took the hat around and was torn between amusement and contempt at the drunken jokes of the farm hands. Gerain was on hand to make sure these didn't go too far, but after the first show, as they were counting the meagre take in the barn, he said, "I don't like this. It's not right, asking Pip to go among them all the time. She's been brought up at court, and this lot are really rough."

"Nonsense," said Josquin. "No one's going to touch her dressed like that."

Both Philippa and Maria were still in the breeches and jerkins that Josquin had found for them when they were hiding.

"It would be better if she were part of the act," Gerain said firmly. "Is there nothing else she can do?"

"Thank you for your kind concern, but I'm capable of speaking for myself!" said Philippa crossly. "If you must know, I can play the harpsichord pretty well, because I used to accompany Maria when she was practising."

"She's not at all bad," confirmed Maria.

"But we haven't got a harpsichord. And even if we found one we could hardly tuck it into a rucksack until we get to the next venue." Josquin looked up from the small pile of coins he had been counting. "Anyway, if tonight's anything to go by, we're soon going to be out of business. There's barely enough here to cover one square meal. The trouble is that we don't offer a varied enough show. We need clowns, a play perhaps, acrobats . . . A fortune-teller." He looked at Philippa.

She shook her head, slowly.

"And the juggling – can't you *vary* it a little, Ger? They've all seen three balls in the air a thousand times. Most of the audience could probably do as well themselves," Josquin said.

"What about this?" Gerain threw three apples in the air and kept them aloft as he turned round, balanced along a beam and jumped off the other side.

Josquin sighed. "A bit better," he conceded. "Now, if you could get an act going with Pip, with scythes or burning swords . . . I saw one chap once set his own hair alight—"

"No way."

"All right," said Philippa. "I'll tell fortunes. If you insist. But I'm not going to do it for real, I'm just going to tell people vague and comforting stories—"

"That's fine, that's great." Josquin leant back against a bale of hay, his arms clasped behind his head. "Just so long as you remember, all girls without a wedding ring want one, and all women with one would rather be rid of it. Especially if they've lots of children . . . The men will want to know about money, deals and so on . . . advise caution, and you won't get caught out. Talk about people crossing water, and tall strangers and falling stars . . . You can do it, I'm sure. It's not at all hard. All you have to do is convince them that you believe it yourself."

"Is that what you do when you act?" asked Maria curiously.

"I suppose so . . . you just have to think what it's really like to be inside someone else's skin . . . what do they feel, what did they have for breakfast, do their shoes hurt, and what do they *want?* It's not hard."

Philippa frowned. This was deception of the most subtle, insidious kind. "We haven't got time to rehearse, I suppose?"

"I thought that we were meant to be on the run," said Maria. "How far do we have to go now?"

"To the lake?" Josquin shook his head. "Weeks, two at least. I can't really remember. We didn't go there often. Not much in the way of audiences, you see. It's a wilderness, that part of Soprafini. Wolves, bears . . . some people say it's haunted."

"I've had enough of these 'hauntings'. It's all hearsay. We saw no sign of that child who died in the water chute, did we?" Maria wrapped her cloak more warmly around her feet. "Anyway, I'm getting cold. Where are our rooms?"

"You see them around you, lady," Josquin said. "The farmer said we could stay here and help ourselves to milk in the morning—"

"Sleep *here?* On all this – hay?"

"It's better than out in the open, surely. It can be very comfortable, lady. You'll see." Philippa spent some time fussing around Maria before settling herself for the night.

All the time she was preoccupied by memories of her vision. She thought, did I see the child who died in the water chute? Was that who she was? But what does she want? Why am I all wrong, the wrong person for her? The vision had been too brief, too mysterious. It seemed insoluble.

Later that night, unable to sleep, Philippa rolled over and pulled on her cloak. The other three were all fast asleep.

A half-moon shone over the farmyard. All was quiet. Far off she heard the melancholy call of an owl. At one corner of the barn was a water barrel. She leaned over the top, and the half-moon smiled back at her from the dark depths.

In that darkness she saw walls and roofs. The moon was shining over a town, a riverside town Philippa didn't recognize. At first, everything was peaceful, the town quiet by the river, the moon gleaming down on it.

But as she watched the moon's tips became

tinged with fire. The orange flickered and snapped, and flames sprang into being. The fire spread outwards from the moon. It became a ring of fire, consuming the quiet little town. Philippa could almost hear the screams of the inhabitants, and something else.

She heard the screams of the Fireflies, howling at her from the depths of the watery screen.

Trembling, she put her hand in the water to disturb its surface. And for a moment she thought she felt the heat, the dreadful burning breath of the Fireflies, biting into her skin.

They followed the river. It wound through agricultural land and at intervals along the route they found dead and dying plants, the corpses of small animals and fish floating belly upwards in the river itself.

"What's happened?" said Maria. "What's gone wrong?" She held in her hand the small corpse of a kingfisher, a brilliant flash of blue and green, dulling already in the morning sun.

"It's the water," said Gerain grimly. "See how it still runs cloudy in the middle . . . poison, pollution of some kind."

"Rustrians," said Philippa a little hollowly. "When we stayed there we were shown their workshops where strange compounds were mixed. People working there wore masks over their noses and mouths. Prince Ferrian told us they could poison the whole of the Western Ocean, if they wanted to."

"Barbarians!" Gerain was outraged. "How dare they?"

"Tell me about those fiery monsters," asked Josquin. "Are they really so dangerous?"

"Dangerous is quite the wrong word for it," said Philippa, shuddering. "Oh, yes, we were shown them. We saw them being fed . . ." She paused. "They have no mouths, only these long snouts. They move terribly quickly, you can hardly see them at all. They kill their prey by breathing fire at them, there's no chance of escape. Only ashes are left . . . Looking back, it seems to me now that Prince Ferrian did everything he could to impress and intimidate us." She looked questioningly at Maria, who nodded agreement. "The Rustrians intend to control the waterlands with poison. Everything else can be reached by Fireflies . . ."

"Is it true that Fireflies can't stand water? That it's like acid to them?"

"Prince Ferrian said they could get round it," said Philippa regretfully. "But it's hard to know why they didn't use them against the Barusi. Water must be a serious problem to the Rustrians."

"The Council always insisted that every entry to the mountain fastness be screened by water," said Gerain. "It might be true . . ."

As they continued along the side of the meandering river, their eyes continually searched the mountains behind them for signs of the Rustrians and their Fireflies.

Somehow, they knew they wouldn't be long in appearing.

They gave performances and gradually the act came together. Sometimes they took advice from the people they played to and turned aside from the main course of the river to find other more remote communities. They scraped a living, and learned some of the tricks of the trade.

The most important thing they learned was how to get along together. It wasn't easy. Maria had regrettable lapses into spoiled princess mode and Gerain was prone to unreasonable depressions.

"Well, wouldn't you be depressed if you'd had to betray a friend?" he flared. They were sitting on a log watching the dying embers of that evening's fire. A barn owl hooted mournfully a little way off. That evening's performance had gone badly, and they had scraped a meagre meal of bread and milk. It was getting very cold at nightfall now. They were all huddled in their cloaks.

"Were you close?" asked Philippa.

Gerain sighed. "Not really. He's a lot older than I am. They wouldn't have chosen him as my guardian otherwise. He was . . . always going off to some meeting or another, always passionate about the cause. At least, that's what I thought. He seemed to be completely obsessed by the arethusans. I really believed that he was doing all this for them. But now I know that he was just out for himself. He wanted to take over the Barusi, become some kind of petty king."

"Did you really have no idea of this?"

"It's difficult to be objective about someone you live with. He looked after me, he brought me up, I was just a child. I never knew my parents. Marco was always in charge."

"I've never lived with anyone like that," said Philippa. "Apart from Maria."

"So you have no family, either." Gerain glanced at her. "Sorry, it's just. . . ."

"It's this question of betrayal, that's what's wrong. You said it yourself," Josquin commented. "That's why it's so upsetting."

"You were lucky, weren't you?" Maria said to him. "Philippa with no family at all, Gerain with his awful guardian and my parents – well,

I never really knew them. You were the only one of us to have a real family life, although no one could call it ordinary."

"I can't wait to find Miracule again," said Josquin. "It's bound to happen again one day, especially now that they know we'll be coming this way. And we're getting a real act together now. Miracule might even give us a separate billing."

Full of pleasant dreams of applause and acclaim, they curled up on the heathery ground and tried to sleep.

CHAPTER 17

That was the first night of frost. In the morning they were all stiff and sore and their breath showed steamy in the clear air.

Maria did not complain, but Philippa spoke for them all. "We need to find shelter tonight," she said. "A town, or a village. I don't want another night out in the open."

They gathered everything together and began to tramp along the track which ran beside the river. The ground was hard beneath their boots, and they were all hungry. By the end of the morning, they were all extremely relieved to find smoke wreathing on the horizon.

It was with high hopes that they entered

Lowenbridge. A sign painted on a broken gate told them the town's name.

It stood at the side of the river, a haphazard jumble of buildings leading down to a quayside. The river was sluggish here, a deep brown colour. But the poison seemed to have run its course and they saw no dead fish washing up against the quay. There was no one much around, just a few grubby children playing in the dust, an old man sitting on a bench in the sun.

From the river, Lowenbridge was a squalid, depressing place. The air was sour with the stink of rotten vegetation and worse. Most of the houses were built in terraces above the level of the water, but the poorest ran straight on to the quay. These were run-down shacks with children squalling in the doorways. A couple of barges were tethered to a frail wooden bridge which just spanned the width of the river. Their paint was cracked and peeling, their woodwork splintering.

Even Josquin was discouraged. "Well, I suppose we'd better ask if we can perform anywhere—"

"There's no money here," said Gerain. "We may as well move on."

"No. We need shelter tonight," said Maria firmly. "Remember?"

Josquin said, "Well, they've got money for

drink. Look." He pointed to a man who was slumped against the door of one of the houses on the quay, half lost in sleep. He was clutching an almost-empty bottle to his chest as if it were a baby. The houses standing on the terraces looked in a marginally better condition. The four travellers turned away from the river and began to climb the steps which led to the first of the terraces.

Nothing. Not a sign of life or movement. The blank faces of houses were shuttered against them. Another set of stairs led to the second terrace and there they found a lurid sign, swinging in the wind. THE GREEN MAN, it said. Doubtfully, they approached it.

The inn was plushly decorated, with red velvet curtains and gilt tassels. Maria, Gerain and Philippa waited outside, kicking their heels in the pale sunlight, while Josquin went in. He had somehow managed to get himself appointed their spokesman. It was something to do with his experience of travelling, of life on the road. He knew how things worked.

Josquin asked the man behind the bar about performing there.

"You're welcome," said the landlord sourly. He put down the glass he was polishing. There was no one else in the bar. "The cockroaches might appreciate a song or two."

"Where is everyone?" asked Josquin.

"Down yonder," he said. "There's some gypsies got an act down by the quay. You'll be wasting your time trying to get work there, they'll take all the custom. I could do with a rival attraction, though." His eyes flickered greedily. "How many of you? What can you do? Now, dancing girls, that would bring them in . . . You haven't got any dancing girls, have you?"

Josquin paused. "Just a moment," he said and went outside to find the others.

"How's your dancing, ladies? The man back there thinks that showgirls might bring in some trade."

"No." Philippa had been looking down over the town, and her face had gone very pale. "Let's leave here. Let's get away from here. I don't like this place, I don't want to stay here."

"What's the matter with it?" asked Gerain in surprise. "It's not up to much, I know. But a booking's a booking—"

"Spoken like a real old trouper," said Josquin approvingly.

Philippa said again, increasingly frantic, "It's not right, I don't like it here, it's too far from the river. Let's try somewhere else."

They all stared at her.

"I saw it in the water!" she cried. "This is a

bad place, there's going to be a fire here, we need to be nearer to the water!"

For once, Philippa could not be budged. She explained what she'd seen in the light of that burning moon. Looking down on it from the terraces, she could see that this was the town encircled by fire. There was no shifting her.

"I suppose we might as well go see what's going on by the river," said Josquin, "before we decide. We'll be safe enough there, you'll agree . . . Water, water everywhere. And besides, we might as well investigate the opposition. We might even learn a few tricks." He sighed. "God knows, we could do with it."

Wearily, they picked their way back down the steps to the river again.

They could hear music and shouting and clapping along the quayside. At one end of it, almost in the river, stood an ancient inn, half-timbered in black and grey-white.

Josquin suddenly halted. "I could swear – yes, that is Aqurelt's voice, I'd know it any-where. It has to be Miracule! We're in luck, chaps, we've come home!"

''What?'' Infected by his enthusiasm, they began to run.

There were people on the pavement, people crowding the doorway, children standing on each others' shoulders, peering in through grimy windows. On the collapsible stage at the end of the main room, a man in turquoise robes span streams of water into exotic patterns while a mermaid sang.

Miracule and the Lady Aqurelt, without a doubt. There was no way through the crowds, but Josquin, practised in the travellers' arts, took them round the back.

In a tiny room, more like a broom cupboard than anything, they found Sylvie.

"Good heavens, Josquin! What brought you here?" She sprang up and kissed him lightly on both cheeks. "You managed to get away then?"

"Oh, Syl, we've had such a time!" He hugged her. "I'm so glad we found you all!"

She batted her eyelashes at him. "We had a terrible time too, getting out of Barusi. We had to go through one of those long passages to the forest, because the Rustrians were roaming everywhere over the top of the mountain! And then we found that some of our things had been stolen, some of the costumes—"

She glanced at Maria and Philippa, who were standing in the doorway, wearing the missing articles. They both looked uncomfortable.

Sylvie pulled away from Josquin. "It was you, you took the stuff! Miracule will be furious with you—"

"No he won't." Josquin grinned at the others. Gerain nodded, almost imperceptibly. "Look Syl, we need work. We've got no money—"

"I thought she's supposed to be a princess!" Sylvie flicked a glance at Maria.

"Temporarily without funds," said Maria shortly. She was brittle and touchy.

Josquin continued. "We're out of Barusi now, there are no Rustrians here, it wouldn't be dangerous—"

"No Rustrians? Are you out of your mind? This place is crawling with them. It's a Rustrian outpost, the whole town is in hock to the Rustrians." The four fugitives exchanged glances. "Haven't you heard about the quotas? The Rustrians take a third of everything – money, food, firewood, fish . . . It's a tax, they say, so that they can defend the locals against Barusi attack—"

"We never attacked anyone!" Gerain was outraged.

"That's what the Rustrians say," said Sylvie coolly. "Anyway, you'd be mad to stay here. If they don't know now that you've escaped from Barusi, they soon will. There are riders travelling between here and Rienzi all the time."

They had seen no one on the road. Only a few farm carts, nothing more.

"Anyway, there's no spare billing," said Sylvie.

"I've been promoted, and Aqurelt is doing an extra item."

"I need to talk to Miracule," Josquin said.

"Small hope." Sylvie went to the door. "But they'll be finished soon."

And indeed they could hear the roll of drums and delighted gasps that always accompanied the climax to popular acts of magic. They waited until the applause had died away, until the doors to the taproom had opened and closed, and Sylvie was out there, doing her bit.

Miracule and Lady Aqurelt had the room next to Sylvie's. Josquin knocked on the door and opened it without waiting.

"Josquin! My dearest boy!" Miracule's welcome was warmly affectionate. A swirl of blue robes and Josquin was engulfed in his arms. And then the Lady Aqurelt, softly kissing his cheeks, although her eyes were shadowy with anxiety.

"I can't pretend not to be glad to see you, Josquin, but this is madness! I would never have accepted a booking here if I'd known. It's quite unsafe. This is a very bad place." Miracule sat them down on trunks and boxes scattered around the room. Aqurelt seated herself at the mirror, and watched them all reflected there.

"We need to work," said Josquin plainly. "We need to join a company."

"Can't carry it on your own?" Miracule paused. "We can't help you lads, ladies . . . not here. You need to move on, go anywhere else but here. . . ."

"There are Rustrians in the audience every night." Lady Aqurelt paused in the act of wiping off make-up. She turned round, waving a cotton-wool ball at them. "They're pretending to be off duty, but I don't think Rustrian soldiers are ever *truly* off duty. I knew them right away, all those shaven heads!"

Without her make-up, the strong lines of her face were emphasized. She looked almost frightening and Philippa wondered for a moment if perhaps she was really a mermaid. But beneath the shiny sequined green dress, two silver slippers peeped, ordinary, high-heeled and built to carry an ordinary human being.

"Can I have a quick look?" Philippa went to the door.

Lady Aqurelt went with her.

They returned after only a minute, and Philippa's face was ashen.

"There are dozens of them!" she said to Maria and the others. "At every exit, at every window. You'd think they ran the place, the way they behave."

They stared at each other. In the silence they

heard the Caccini brothers doing their drumming act.

"Blast it!" Miracule suddenly made up his mind. "Am I man or mouse? Should I turn away my brother's son? Of course you can stay with us, dear boy, you and all your friends!" He swung wide his arms. "We can outwit a bunch of Rustrian thugs, don't you worry!"

"But you'll have to be part of the act, right away, or it will look like a put-up job. Get out there, Jos. On stage." Aqurelt spoke quickly. "Here, take this—"

She held out a scarlet cloak to him and a feathered mask on a stick. "Do your act with the Caccini. It's only our second night, we can pretend you were here all the time, sick or something yesterday. We'll say you've been with us all along. And you – Princess Maria? – you sing, don't you? Sylvie can find you a wig, a dress. Drat, where is the girl?"

She looked round anxiously, but there was no sign of Sylvie. "She ought to be here, I don't like the way she keeps slipping off . . . Never mind, we'll have to make do. Get ready. You're on next." She smiled suddenly. "This is all in the best theatrical tradition, my dears. Don't be nervous. You'll be splendid!"

For a moment Maria gaped at her. And then Aqurelt whisked a deep-dyed aquamarine dress from a trunk and held it up against her. "This will have to do, although Sylvie's might fit you better. Such a shame about your hair," she said, "but no one need know—"

Gerain and Philippa, pushed out into the corridor with Miracule, looked through the curtains behind the bar. They saw Josquin, the mask held steadily in front of his face, gracefully balancing along a low-rope to the drumming accompaniment as if he'd been doing it all his life . . . which he certainly had, thought Philippa.

She looked beyond them, scanning the faces in the crowd. It was easy enough to make out the Rustrians. They were lounging in the doorways, heavily armed. Large, hard-faced men in brilliant, gaudy uniforms. They made no pretence of watching the show. Their eyes ceaselessly moved between the stage, audience, and exits. One of them glanced at a poster announcing Miracule's troupe. He said something to his companions and only then did they laugh. One of them moved a little closer to the stage.

"What do the posters say?" Philippa asked Miracule.

"Nothing specific," he replied. "Just the main acts, and 'supporting cast'. We're covered; we might just get away with it."

"But there's a traitor here! Someone let them know we were here—"

"Where *is* Sylvie?" asked Aqurelt sharply.

"Are you accusing me?" Sylvie was standing by the dressing-room door, her curls hanging straight and heavy, wet with rain. Her mascara was leaving black rivulets down her cheeks. "I just stepped outside for some fresh air when they jumped me! The innkeeper at the Green Man reported you, it wasn't me!"

"Why should we believe you?" Gerain was cold. He was remembering the way Marco and his men had found them so quickly in Barusi. Sylvie hadn't been around then, either.

"Look." She pulled off her cloak and they saw the bruises on her arm already darkening. "Do you think I got these by accident – they arrested me, I tell you. They had so many questions . . . I tried to defend you, I said you were members of our troupe, always had been!" She turned from one to the other of them. "Why won't you believe me? I did my best!"

"And they would surely have arrested us right away, wouldn't they?" Maria said unwillingly. "The fact that we're still here must mean that she's telling the truth."

"Right." Miracule had made up his mind. "You're members of the Players. If we keep our heads, we can make something of this. The princess here sings, and Josquin's an old hand. But what are we going to do with the

Lady Philippa? And our friend Gerain here? How are you going to contribute to our merry band?"

"I tell fortunes," said Philippa glumly. "And Gerain can juggle, a bit. Or he takes the hat round."

"We can find him something more interesting than that. Straight man to Rafael, perhaps . . ." Miracule's sharp little eyes were thoughtful. "We shall contrive, my dears, we shall contrive."

CHAPTER 18

Miracule's troupe was booked for seven nights at the Pig and Whistle, but they didn't complete the run.

Rustrians came to every performance, and Philippa found herself in contact with them all the time. She sat in a booth in the squalid courtyard of the inn before the matinee next day and told fortunes.

The word went round and the queue lengthened. Even the Rustrians seemed to want their fortunes told, although they took little notice of what she said.

Philippa wore veils and heavy dress jewellery borrowed from Aqurelt and did her best to appear mysterious, but still she wondered why everyone wanted to hear what she had to say. She quite enjoyed inventing tales of lost lovers, of malicious enchantments and curses. "You've been unlucky," she said, and everyone responded to this with enthusiasm, even the Rustrians.

The odd thing was that sometimes Philippa felt that she really did know what was going to happen. Whenever she spoke to the ordinary townspeople she knew she was telling the truth. The water showed her over and over again the same scene, a scene of utmost violence and destruction. It was going to take place here, in Lowenbridge. She'd seen it.

It happened on that very first day. Philippa had just hung the sign outside the tent. She was still arranging herself and the props when the flap was pushed open. The woman stared suspiciously around. She was pale and thin, and carried a baby in a sling on her back, holding two other toddlers by the hand. With difficulty she squeezed into the tent and dropped a coin into the bowl of water on the table. She sat down and waited patiently, while her children began to roam everywhere, pulling at things, investigating.

And as the ripples cleared, Philippa saw that same, undeniable picture. The picture she'd seen in that moonlit water-barrel, the half moon eaten by fire. . . .

She saw flames and fire ripping through the town where they stood. Destruction, the houses tumbling in piles of charred timbers. "If I were you, I'd leave here immediately," she said, her eyes gazing directly at the woman. "Take your children and get out of here."

"What? What are you saying?" The woman looked irritated. "Look, I wanted to know about my man, whether he's seeing that woman down the road—"

"He isn't," Philippa said with certainty. That was going to be the least of the woman's worries. "But whether he is or not, you must leave this place. It's more than urgent, it's a matter of life and death."

There was something in her tone which stopped the woman in her tracks. She blinked. "Well, I was thinking of going to see my sister in the mountains before the snows set in—"

"Do so. Don't delay." Philippa sighed with relief as the woman gathered up her children and made for the exit. "Oh, lady—"

The woman paused. "Tell your friends," said Philippa. "Tell everyone you know."

The woman looked as if Philippa were mad. But gradually, during the length of that long afternoon, as she repeated her vision over and over again to the townspeople, Philippa saw carts and wagons, heavily laden with bundles

222

and children and animals pull away from the village. The audience for that evening show was rather sparse.

She went on repeating her message.

But the Rustrians paid no attention at all.

"I wish I knew what they wanted. Why they're watching us," she commented next day. "I suppose they know who we are—"

"Well, why haven't they arrested us?" Maria was preening herself in one of Sylvie's costumes. She had enjoyed the previous evening's performance, the shouts and the applause. Someone had thrown flowers at her. The audience's approval had nothing to do with the flattery she had received at court. This audience would have had no hesitation in throwing rotten eggs if she hadn't pleased them.

For the first time, Maria was experiencing some pride in herself which was not the result of her position.

"I don't know why they haven't arrested us . . ." said Philippa, frowning. "They're waiting for something, and there's these visions I keep seeing . . . Can't we move on? I don't like it here, not at all!"

But Miracule insisted that they stay to the end of the booking. "The show must go on, my dear," he said, a little sadly. "We cannot possibly back out of a contract, we'll never get asked back. And it would look so suspicious. They'd be after us right away. I'd let you go on separately, but I really think your chances will be better under our protection."

He was an old man, experienced in the ways of the world. All of them knew that their best chances were with him and his troupe. Nowhere else would they find such excellent cover.

Philippa had spent the break between performances altering Maria's costume so that it fitted better. The fortune-telling trade had dropped off slightly. She must have told close on a hundred fortunes, she thought, but no one came back a second time. Most of them had left town.

Maria had been rehearsing with Josquin and Sylvie, learning how to project her voice.

"It takes years to learn how to be audible in a noisy taproom," said Josquin encouragingly. "Singing in private halls to respectful courtiers must be a very different affair. No one's going to flatter you here . . ." And those clear grey eyes gleamed at her. "You're doing very well, really you are."

Maria preened herself.

Gerain was studying a map of the region which Miracule had lent him. He looked up. "I wish I knew what those Rustrians were after," he said. "I don't understand what they're all doing here if they're not looking for us. And if they are looking for us, why haven't we been arrested?"

"I'll see if I can find out what they're after," said Josquin. He was high and reckless on the evening's success.

His act with Sylvie had been a wild, rip-roaring show-stopper. People were coming from the outer villages, drawn by the drama of it. They performed scenes from a well-known tragedy. The meeting of young lovers, their despair at their respective families' disapproval. The sword fight between Josquin and Sylvie's stage father (Miracule, in velvet and lace). The death of the father, the remorse of the suitor, the removal of the heroine to a nunnery and her subsequent demise . . . It was a favourite story, and had been set to music by Miracule himself.

The story alone, popular though it was, would not have been enough to draw such an audience. But Miracule's music made use of simple, catchy melodies, played against the drumming accompaniment of the two Caccini brothers, those experts in the complications of higher mathematics. Every emotion in the play was caught and amplified by their off-beat, excitable rhythms. It was a rare audience that didn't find itself dancing at some point during the performance.

That second evening they had had to give three encores of the finale. Maria's solo spot early in the second half had also received enthusiastic applause. She was very pleased with herself. When Josquin offered to find out what the Rustrians wanted, she thought he was joking.

"How? Are you going to take up eaves-dropping?"

"I don't see why not. We need to know whether they're just keeping a general eye on this area or whether they really are looking for us. Whether they're going to keep hounding Miracule's troupe. It's sensible to find out, don't you think?"

"I suppose so . . ." Maria said doubtfully.

"So, who's game? Who fancies a spot of night-walking?" He was a little drunk on the beer the inn supplied free to the performers. "Are the Rustrians still in the bar?"

Looking through the curtain, Philippa saw that they were indeed still there, but on the point of leaving.

Josquin stood up. "Coming, Ger?"

Maria got to her feet too. "I'd like to see what these people want—"

"Lady Maria, your Royal Highness, I don't wish to exclude anyone, and I'm sure that you're just as good (if not better) than I am at creeping through the dark—". Maria threw a bread roll at him, " – but I think you should stay home and look after yourself. Performers of the feminine persuasion need to nurture themselves, to relax and have a good twelve hours' beauty sleep—"

"Rubbish!" said Philippa. "But a great crowd of us trying to be quiet and unobtrusive is a non-starter. You'd probably be more successful on your own."

"I don't like this at all," said Maria. "If it's too dangerous for us, what makes it safe for you?"

"Can you throw an accurate knife, lady? Defend yourself against armed men? Well, can you?" said Gerain.

"I've been around. It's not all water-colours and courtly dancing on the road." He was laughing at her, not in the least subdued. "You're just jealous you might miss all the fun."

She knew that under the joking he was perfectly serious. "Idiot. But you *do* have to perform too. Take care."

Josquin was pulling his sleeves down to cover the lacy cuffs, winding a dark scarf round his neck, blackening his face with stage make-up. He helped Gerain do the same. Maria and Philippa watched them in silence.

"Goodnight, sweet ladies," Josquin sketched an elaborate bow. "Be good . . ." He left the inn with Gerain.

*　　*　　*

"On your own, girls?" The Lady Aqurelt had entered their dressing room. She was carrying a tray. On it, light from a tall ivory candle glinted on crystal glasses and a filigree silver flagon. She put the tray down on the dressing table and turned down the gas lamps. From one of her capacious pockets she drew a small silver casket.

"Now," she said, lowering her generous bulk on to the velvet cushions that were part of the props for the play. "A midnight feast, I thought . . . a few treats to while away the time until those boys get back." She beamed at them. "A little Camberai wine, my dears? Seaweed crackers?"

These were delicacies famed throughout Soprafini but rarely tasted, even at court. Maria was delighted. She smiled at the lady.

"Where did you get them?" she asked, lifting her glass so that the candlelight shone through the straw-coloured wine. "Oh, this is a *very* good colour!"

"The best." The Lady Aqurelt nodded comfortably. "A gift from the Lydian Emperor. He was in love with me for a time—" She smiled. "You may find it hard to believe, but once I was really *very* beautiful—"

"And although modesty is not one of my lady's many shining virtues, she is not exaggerating."

Miracule twinkled at them round the door. He came in, laden with more substantial refreshments: patés, crusty bread, baby tomatoes and courgettes stewed in oil. The Caccini brothers arrived next with the smelliest cheese that Philippa and Maria had ever encountered. They explained earnestly that the smell was an indication of its venerable age and worth, and fell over laughing, rolling on the floor, at Maria's face when she tried it.

Ruby the contortionist brought her pet snake Diana in and let her wreath around everyone's shoulders. This was disconcerting, but not unpleasant. Diana's skin was dry and textured like a sequinned bag, and beautifully patterned. Ruby had a basket of plums with her and more wine.

Everyone shrieked with laughter as she told jokes and sang a comic song, poking fun at the way Miracule ate his food, and then the innkeeper came and joined in. He took one look at Diana round Philippa's neck and nearly fainted. He needed beer to revive him and so that started to flow as well.

It was a great party, the kind of party that only takes place when things are on the edge. At the back of everyone's mind the Rustrians waited, watching for any slip. They were all conscious, all the time, that Josquin and Gerain had not returned.

But at last most of them had drifted away to bed, and Miracule and Aqurelt were left with a very anxious Maria and Philippa. Miracule looked at his lady, cleared his throat, and said "Dears, if ever you want a home, somewhere to stay, for as long as you want . . . I hope you don't think this presumptuous, my dear princess, but one can never foresee what surprises life may bring . . . you can always come with us. You'll always be welcome here, whenever, whatever. . . ."

They smiled at him affectionately as he left the dressing room. The Lady Aqurelt did not go with him.

She sat down again, a little heavily, on the dressing table stool. She no longer looked quite so relaxed. Gerain and Josquin's absence could no longer be disregarded.

The Lady Aqurelt began to speak. "My dears, I join Miracule in everything he has said, but I think a few explanations are due. Miracule is so glad to have Josquin back, so appreciative of your voice, my lady, so glad to have you all with us, that I think he is not being altogether sensible . . ." She paused. "What are you hoping to achieve?" she asked.

There was a silence. In the end, it was Philippa who replied. "We're going to Lake Ere."

"Indeed?" Aqurelt looked at her calmly. There was something in her expression that Philippa could not understand. She sounded calm, but her emerald eyes showed something else. "Forgive my lack of understanding, but why? There's nothing there, no towns, no *people*. What will you do?"

"We weren't going there to perform," Philippa said.

"These visions you see . . ." said the Lady Aqurelt, as if it were the most ordinary thing in the world. "These things you are warning the townspeople about, they're not just stories, are they? You are an aquemancer, my dear, aren't you?"

And so it all came out, all about that great lake draining away and revealing. . . .

"Well, just what *is* revealed?" Maria said at last. "You keep going on about some great secret, Pip, but you never say what it is."

"I can't!" Philippa felt almost like crying. "It's not my secret, it belongs to someone else." She was very tired, more than a little worried about the others and she hated talking about this, hated revealing these visions in this way.

The Lady Aqurelt was looking at her again in that strange, understanding way. "Don't let anyone bully you, my Philippa," she said. "It's enough that people should believe there's something of significance there. Mysteries are not made to be gossiped about."

"Anyway," said Philippa. "It doesn't really matter if there's anything significant there or not. The dam has to be destroyed so that the Ere can flow to the sea again. That way, the arethusans are going to survive. That's why Gerain is willing to go along with this."

Aqurelt's strange green eyes were suddenly withdrawn, secretive. She nodded slowly. Then she turned to Maria. "And what about you, my lady? Why do you want to go to Lake Ere?"

Maria hesitated. "There's nowhere else," she said at last. "I can't go back to Rustria because I can't bear to marry Ferrian. And I can't go home because I've let them down so. They're so frightened of Rustria! I don't know if my parents will ever forgive me."

"Parents always forgive," said Aqurelt. "It comes with the job."

"Not always," said Maria bleakly. "Not when they're in charge of thousands of people and have to put the greater good first."

"It wasn't fair on you," said Philippa.

"It's not fair on all those people in Soprafini. They've got the Rustrians leeching everything from them, and the constant threat of war." Maria spoke angrily.

"You never used to worry about it before,"

observed Philippa.

"That was before. I hadn't seen much, then."

A small silence. Aqurelt dropped her hand on Maria's shoulder, a gentle reassurance. "You've come a long way," she said.

Looking at Maria, Philippa knew it was the exact truth.

They were still talking when Sylvie burst into the room.

She was chalk-white. "It's Josquin!" she said. "He's been hurt—"

And then Gerain came stumbling through the door, supporting Josquin, whose legs seemed dangerously unsteady. He collapsed into a chair, his hand clasped to his shoulder. "Filthy Rustrians . . ." he said. "Should have known they'd be waiting—"

Philippa saw a spreading stain of red on Josquin's shoulder. "Did you have to be a hero?"

Through the black greasepaint, she could see that his face was grey. "A hero? Oh, no. There was no heroism in it at all. We just followed those soldiers by the door, quietly, we were really quiet you know. . . ."

"Unfortunately," said Gerain, "in Josquin's efforts to discover why we weren't arrested days ago, one of the Rustrians met with a fatal accident. . . ."

As Lady Aqurelt pulled out her medical kit, they explained what had happened.

The barman said that the Rustrians had barracks on the north side of the town, on the terraces above the harbour. Josquin and Gerain had slipped along the quay, past the shabby, rusty fishing-boats which lurked in the dark. They had turned a corner and almost walked straight into a group of Rustrians, enjoying a late evening smoke and drink on the quayside.

They'd hung back in the shadows, trying to listen to the conversation but learned nothing. "And then this wretched cat yowled," said Gerain furiously. "They all looked round and saw us there, and then the weapons were out, swords and knives – we ran. What else could we do?" He looked round at them all. "We dodged down the alleys, ran up the terraces behind the town . . . but there were too many of them. They separated and then we were cornered. It was a close thing."

For a moment he watched Aqurelt dab lotion on Josquin's shoulder. "One of them nearly caught Josquin. We saw them coming and got up on to a wall—"

"The human fly . . ." said Josquin faintly. "You should have seen him move. . . ."

"You were right behind me. Anyway, we were running along the top of this wall, and one of the Rustrians tried to follow. Stupid. The man fell. He broke his neck."

"Are you sure?" Aqurelt said sharply.

"I stopped and looked back. I had to know—" Gerain looked very sick. "His head – was all twisted, all wrong. We were running then, but the other Rustrians were waiting for us. One of them must have been practising. He threw his knife and caught Josquin in the shoulder. But we were ahead then, and we lost them round the terraces. . . ."

Josquin's eyes closed momentarily. Aqurelt was both careful and gentle, but the knife wound went deep. "That Rustrian would have made a good performer," he said, trying a smile, but it didn't work. "Quite an eye, he had. . . ."

"Hush . . ." The Lady Aqurelt was competently tearing some linen into strips. Maria watched, with a horrid sort of fascination.

"Come on." Philippa took Maria by the hand, attempting to pull her from the room.

"No, let me be . . ." Maria went to the table and poured some water into a bowl. "Can I help, Lady Aqurelt? Is there anything I can do?"

Aqurelt barely glanced at her. "Go and heat

up some water," she said shortly. "To boiling. Then you must hold the bowl steady—"

And then even Philippa, watching, forgot who Maria was.

CHAPTER 19

Such a long night. Josquin tossed and turned, trying hard to keep a grip on things, but the combination of pain and fever were too much. Aqurelt and Maria took turns to be with him, and no one slept well.

But by the morning, Josquin's eyes were clear, his pulse steadier. He smiled weakly as Philippa brought rolls and coffee.

"How are you feeling?" she asked.

"Sick as a cushion." He grinned, ruefully. "Can Gerain be understudy?"

It was half a joke, but they all saw the seriousness of the point.

"I can't possibly," said Gerain.

For a moment, they regarded him. Tall, dark-haired, broad shouldered . . . he was opposite to Josquin in every way. He was serious, moody . . . he had none of Josquin's lightness, his grace. It was impossible to imagine Gerain serenading Sylvie, sword-fighting with Miracule. He was not in the least musical, and incapable of acting anything other than himself.

"Too honest," sighed Miracule. "Not enough fantasy. It won't do, it won't do at all."

They stared at each other, nonplussed. Everyone knew that the Rustrians would be there again that night. They would expect the same show, the same cast to sing, dance and caper.

"I'll do it," said Josquin. "I can manage."

"Of course you can't!" Even Sylvie was outraged. "You'll never get through it!"

"What alternative have we?" he asked, and for once there was no sign of a smile or a joke.

And so that evening's show went ahead.

The Rustrians were there, of course. They lounged by the door, not drinking much, their eyes sharp and critical.

Aqurelt rubbed rouge into Josquin's cheeks. She draped his cloak so that his left arm and shoulder were largely concealed. "Thank heavens it's not the right," she muttered, pulling the bandages tight. "Now, stay sitting wherever possible, lean on chairs, on door frames, *don't* attempt to move quickly whatever you do. . . ."

He nodded, his eyes bright with excitement.

The show began. Philippa, sick with nerves, sat in her kiosk outside the inn, and dipped her hands into the bowl of water.

She heard the applause that concluded Miracule and Aqurelt's spot, the gasps and groans that accompanied Riccardo's fire-eating act. And then the Caccini brothers started their drumming and she stared into the dark water in her cupped hands.

Again, a hand passed over the lake and the waters rolled back. And gleaming there were bones, shining, spiky as stars.

Touched with blood now, tinged with red. Or was it flame, burning the bones, turning them to ash?

Fireflies, she thought. The Lake. The bones and the Fireflies. . . .

The combination nagged at her. What are we getting into, she wondered? What will we be stirring up here? She let the water drain away and went to watch the show.

Josquin's costume was red and black. His face, beneath its garish make-up was bright, slightly sweaty. He moved with all the usual grace, all the usual verve and energy, and they all knew it could not last.

If he collapsed, the Rustrians would investigate. They would find the knife wound, they would remember the young man who had run along the top of a wall, leaving one of their number to die.

They would be furious, out for revenge. They would take Josquin, and then all the rest of them.

In the wings, Gerain fingered one of the stage swords, wondering if it could be sharpened. He could hear Josquin's voice, a little quieter than usual, but keeping up well with the music. He realized, listening carefully, that the drums were subdued. The Caccini brothers were doing their best to adapt.

"Come live with me, the world loves lovers—" sang Josquin, clasping Sylvie to his breast. Her hands moved, clutching his shirt, and only Maria, watching in the wings, saw the shadow cross his face.

Now the final aria of the first scene. Josquin was down on one knee to Sylvie, his hand pressed to his heart. It was the final bid to tempt the heroine to elope. But his hand was not on his heart, it had moved to his shoulder and Philippa drew in her breath sharply to see the blood welling between his fingers. Sylvie!

she thought. Sylvie, clutching his clothes and reopening the wound. It had to be deliberate. It had to be. . . .

And there was still so much of the piece to go, including the swordfight . . . Miracule suddenly emerged out of the darkness at her side.

"He can't do the swordfight, he's bleeding again!" she whispered to him.

"I know." His lined old face was determined. "We'll do a duel. Fisticuffs, instead. He can keep his arms close, that way. We'll be careful, don't worry."

In the brief change of scene which preceded the duel, Aqurelt rebound Josquin's shoulder while Sylvie, white and shaking, insisted that she hadn't meant to do it, it was an accident, she wouldn't have hurt him for anything, she'd just forgotten he was injured, he was managing so well. . . .

Josquin's blue eyes considered her. "You always were a clumsy one, Syl. It wasn't your fault."

And then they were on again, and the altered dialogue was improvised, to take into account the change from swords to fists.

Philippa and Maria couldn't bear to watch. They sat together in Miracule's dressing room, desultorily turning over the paste jewellery on Aqurelt's dressing table.

"I'm sure she did it deliberately," Maria said. "She knew as well as any of us what was at stake. Even Sylvie is not that stupid."

"But why? Why didn't she just give us away, if she means so much harm?" It seemed insoluble. And then it struck Philippa. She remembered that blood in her vision, the blood that had turned to flame, and the knowledge of the Fireflies.

She paled suddenly. "I know why no one's arrested us. They're waiting for the Fireflies to arrive. They're on their way, and the Rustrians *know* we can't get away. It's why we're being watched so carefully."

Maria's eyes were enormous. "Oh, no!"

"They're just keeping us here, like prisoners, and enjoying the show at the same time! Listen!" In the charged hush from the stage, as the hero discovers the heroine's body, they heard the rattle of ironmongery, the rumble of wheels over stone, the shouts of men.

And a deep, deadly roaring noise, like fire rushing through a house, a street, a city.

Fireflies.

CHAPTER 20

"Bring the curtain down," said the Lady Aqurelt. "You must get out of here immediately."

Everyone was crammed into Miracule's tiny dressing room. As soon as the play finished and Josquin, staggering with weariness, had collapsed off-stage, Aqurelt had gathered them together.

Miracule bundled the fugitives into the dressing room, where Philippa told them what she'd heard.

"I'll go and check." Gerain left the dressing room and pushed his way through the crowds to the stairs. He ran up them three at a time.

When he returned, one look at his face told it all.

The town was surrounded. Hundreds of Rustrian soldiers were ranged over the hills behind the terraces, stationed at every cross-roads, every junction. He'd seen their pale uniforms glinting in torchlight everywhere. And with them, still enclosed in their strange watery cages, the Fireflies howled.

"They're looking for us," said Maria desperately, and no one argued the point.

"Let's see if we can get over the river," said Josquin. "We might have a chance that way. . . ."

They crept out of the inn and made for the bridge.

It was useless. Torchlight flared around them. There were soldiers swarming everywhere, going from house to house along the terraces. Over fifty were stationed on or around the bridge itself.

No way out, no way through. The towns-people were all being herded together into a large square beyond the quayside while their houses were being searched. And then, as they hesitated at the door to the inn, they realized with horror that the Fireflies were being re-leased. With a clang, the cage-doors were opened and fizzing like unstable fuses, the Fire-flies darted out into the town. As ever, they moved too fast, too irregularly, to be seen clearly.

Like an enormous living creature, the crowd drew itself together in the square, moaning. Around it there was an impression of small, dark red eyes flickering, of voracious malevolence. The soldiers in the square operated hoses to keep the Fireflies away from the townspeople.

The monsters turned their attention elsewhere. Their path through the town was marked by falling drips of ash as at every movement they incinerated their surroundings. The stink of burning filled the air.

Wood caught first: doors and window-frames and sheds. An unwary cat was roasted in an explosive flare as it tried to scramble up on to a roof. The roof itself began to smoulder, to char and the Fireflies clustered around it like children at a party.

They capered and scampered and fizzed, wildly out of control.

The crowd was on the edge of panic. There were screams as they saw their homes and their possessions all disappearing as one house after another caught light. The night was split by the cries of people and the crackle of flames.

Miracule's Players took one look at each other and made for the inn, dashing back towards the quay. "Thank goodness you got so many to leave," said Maria to Philippa as they ran. "This is hell, a real hell. . . ."

In a mass they rounded the end of the row of buildings next to the inn.

There was a Firefly blocking their way.

It didn't see them at first. Its attention was focused on the inn sign, swinging creakily above the front door. A moment's grace, while it sent tongues of flame to devour the sign. It swung there for a moment, the paint blistering, before falling to the ground.

The roof timbers caught next. Clouds of smoke began to thread through the tiles.

During the pause most of the Players managed to rush down the alley to the side and get in through the back door to the inn.

But Josquin was moving slowly and awkwardly by this time, exhausted by the run, and Miracule had stayed behind to help him. They didn't dare look back, and the first they knew of the Firefly's presence in the alley with them, was the blast of flame which incinerated the door in front of their eyes.

They span round and the Firefly screamed with delight. It seemed to fill the narrow alley, fizzing with demented energy. Tongues of flame blazed through the air towards the roof and windows above. It was like a living firecracker, exploding in all directions, without order or control. There was no possible way round it, and only a high wall behind them.

They clung together. It came closer. A lick of heat singed Miracule's eyebrows, delicate as a scalpel, another blew Josquin's hat from his head. On a breath of fire the hat skidded along the alley in front of them, before disintegrating into a pile of ash.

The Firefly wanted to play.

Inside the inn, Gerain felt the blast of heat at his back as the door burned. "Miracule and Josquin!" he shouted to Aqurelt, some way ahead. "It's got them!"

"Come with me!" Aqurelt seized Philippa's hand. "This way!" She leapt up the stairs like a young girl, and pushed open one of the bedroom doors. Gerain and the Caccini brothers were just behind.

"Water is the only defence!" gasped Philippa. "We need water!" The Caccinis turned back to the taproom, and began to pass buckets along a chain of the others in the troupe.

Out of the window, Aqurelt and Philippa saw Miracule and Josquin pinned against the wall below. Miracule's cloak was scorched at the shoulder and there was a nasty burn on the side of his neck. They could see that both he and Josquin were sweating in the enormous heat emanating from the Firefly. It was blocking their movement to either side with great bursts of flames. They were helpless, caught like meat on a spit.

The Firefly was too busy concentrating on its prey to notice what was happening above. It began to amuse itself by shooting flame at Miracule and Josquin's feet. They jumped and dodged, but it was desperate.

The first splash of water fell uselessly on the cobbles between the Firefly and Josquin. Not a drop reached the Firefly, it was too far away. It looked up at the window and a plume of flame reached towards Aqurelt and Philippa.

They ducked down, but the top of Aqurelt's hair was singed. Gerain passed them another bucket, and they threw it without daring to stand up. Again, the water fell short.

"No!" Philippa seized the next bucket and tipped the contents directly on to Josquin and Miracule. They staggered under the shock, and the Firefly screamed. Another bucket of water over the two men and the wall beside them, and the flames drew back.

Jos and Miracule began to edge along the wall. The Firefly was backing off, making that terrible high-pitched shriek. It would not go near them if there was water around, but it could call for help. Philippa heard shouts and then the rush of heavy boots over the cobbles. The Rustrians were coming.

Jos and Miracule fell through the blackened hole which had been the back door. "This way." Aqurelt was waiting for them. Grim-faced, she led them all into the tiny back dressing room and locked the door.

It seemed a futile precaution. They could hear the shouts of the Rustrians and the screams of Fireflies just outside.

"What can we do? Should we give ourselves up?" Maria looked frantically at her friends.

"No. Absolutely not," said Aqurelt. "You'll be thrown to the Fireflies. No, we're getting out of here."

"Easier said than done." Josquin was by the window.

Although it was deep night, the sky was hectic with orange fire. In the glow from the window, Josquin's face looked almost healthy. He leaned back against the wall, his eyes closed.

"There is an alternative . . ." The Lady Aqurelt spoke softly. "Shall we, dear?"

This was to Miracule. He took her hand and pressed it. "That's right, lady," he said. "Time to come clean."

"What do you mean?" Josquin opened his eyes and stared from one to the other. "What are you talking about?"

"Come with me." The Lady Aqurelt stood up, swirling her cloak around her generous form. She went to the large mirror hanging on the wall. They watched in puzzlement as she passed her hands over it, muttering something under her breath.

Miracule watched her, his eyes gleaming with pride. He was a stage magician, a clever and gifted actor. He could hold together a troupe of unlikely talents and put on a show that drew crowds from miles around. But he could do nothing like this.

The silvered surface flickered beneath Aqurelt's fingers. A cloud passed over her reflection and as she muttered something no one understood, the mirror seemed to melt. All at once the silver coalesced, gathering together into a bright and shining key, jutting from a keyhole. Where the mirror had hung, an ancient door now stood in the wall.

Aqurelt laid her hand on the key. "Come along now," she said briskly. "This way. Hurry along, there's not much time."

The door swung open lightly and easily. A flight of stairs led downwards beneath the inn. "Some – um, friends of Aqurelt's told us about this," said Miracule. "They said we could use it, if ever we were in need. . . ."

The Players gathered together their most

essential belongings swiftly and efficiently. Then Miracule led the way down the stairs and they all followed. The Lady Aqurelt waited till everyone had gone through and then shut the door gently behind them, turning the key in the lock. Two more muttered words and the key melted, flowing through the keyhole to the other side.

Any observer in the dressing room would see a shining thread suddenly emerge from a keyhole, flowing out to cover the wall as if it had always been a silvery mirror, hanging there.

Beneath the room, the stairs went far deeper than any cellar. There was a rope slung along the wall to hang on to, and they were all glad of this for the treads were slippery with moisture.

Gradually, the darkness lifted. A faint greenish glow hung around them, coming from no source they could make out. And then they were at the bottom of the stairs and ahead of them a wide underground lake stretched far away.

The waters shone with phosphorescence. Everything gleamed as if in a dream. This was the light that had accompanied their descent. And standing at the edge of the lake, silhouetted against its strangely glowing light, someone was waiting for them.

He stepped forward to meet them, and then

they saw that he was not a man at all. He belonged to the dream, to the glowing light of water. Fur draped his long, lean body, and his hands and feet were webbed. Large emerald eyes considered them. He was an arethusan, standing before them at once so like and so unlike humanity.

The Lady Aqurelt went straight up to him, her arms held wide. They embraced, chattering together like long lost friends. But it was in no language that anyone else could understand. This was a rhythm of syllables and sounds that operated in other terms.

Although Philippa thought that perhaps she'd heard it before, in dreams or from long ago, before she knew the meaning of words. She took a step towards him.

The arethusan turned suddenly and held his hand out to her. Hesitantly, a little shy, Philippa touched it. He drew her close. His other hand cupped the side of her face, the soft fur-like silk stroking her cheek. He spoke again to Aqurelt, but his eyes never left Philippa's face. And then he stepped away and dived gracefully into the green-gold waters beyond.

Philippa raised her hands to her neck, where he had touched her, and found there, caught in the web of her hair like a shell in seaweed, a small knot of pearls woven into a coral clasp.

It was a beautiful thing, the creamy pearls set into the polished orangey-pink. It was carved with faces and starfish and sea-horses, exquisitely done.

"Oh – how lovely!" she exclaimed, turning it over in her hand. "Why did he give to me?"

Miracule said, "It is a family gift. The way an arethusan celebrates the coming of age of a relative . . ." His words were for Philippa, but he looked only at Aqurelt.

Philippa was saying, "But how generous of him, how very kind . . ." She caught the glance between Miracule and Aqurelt. "Why did he give it to me?" she asked, suddenly nervous. "What does it mean?"

The Lady Aqurelt smiled. She looked much younger, as if she had been the one given a present. "Only that he will help you," she said. "He knows the way, he knows what you want to do. And you may trust him with your lives."

"But what about you?" asked Josquin. He was sitting on a rock, his hand pressed to his shoulder. He looked terrible. "What will you do?"

"Oh, we'll survive," said Miracule. "We've been in worse scrapes than this, as you well know. We'll sit it out down here until the coast is clear. It wouldn't be the first time." And looking round, they saw all the Players settling down amongst the rocks, unloading their baggage, beginning to prepare a meal as if this were a perfectly ordinary break on the road.

The phosphorescence rippled round them. They saw that the arethusan was returning, bringing with him another. They were towing a small skiff very like the one they had abandoned so far back. The arethusans remained in the water, their sleek heads bobbing just below the surface and Philippa wondered if it had really happened, that one of them had really been *there*, holding her hand, giving her a present that she now wore in her hair.

The Lady Aqurelt was waiting to say farewell. Philippa hugged her, and felt her warm sea-breath.

"You *are* a mermaid!" she said.

A fleeting smile crossed Aqurelt's face. "Nonsense," she said calmly. "There's no such thing. Now be off with you. You've got a long way to go."

"I don't want to go without you!" Philippa said.

"Oh, we'll meet again, little Philippa. Never fear."

It was impossible to disbelieve her.

They climbed into the boat, and the arethusans pulled them out into the centre of the lake. The current caught them and the skiff began to pick up speed. The arethusans and current worked together to move the small craft along at an amazing rate. Water sprayed up at the bows. It was exhilarating and liberating. Philippa was almost laughing. "The Lady Aqurelt's a mermaid, she's one of them!" she sang.

And she pointed to the arethusan and Josquin said, "Off your head. Out of your mind. Now who's delirious?"

Philippa blushed and dropped her head. Maria stared at her as if she were indeed mad. But Gerain nodded, just once, and his hand found Philippa's and gave it a squeeze.

"I was going to tell you the secret one day," he said, "because you're part of it too, but it looks like you already know most of it."

"What do you mean?"

He dropped his voice and leaned closer to her. She wondered what he was going to say. But then Maria pointed out a shoal of golden merries to the right and the moment was lost.

At last, they were out in the open and the cold night air made them shiver.

Far away in the distance, they could see the smoke and flames flaring from the burning town. The sight brought them all abruptly back to their perilous situation.

"The inn on the terraces will be burned. That's why we couldn't stay there," Philippa said. "I knew there was something wrong about that other inn."

"All those people!" said Maria. "Those poor people!"

"They didn't deserve that, did they?" Gerain said bleakly. "I loathe those Firefly things. Abominations. I wish there was some way of destroying them all, getting rid of the whole damn lot of them."

"There aren't that many," said Maria thoughtfully. "Only two hundred or so. . . ."

"Only! A dozen of them destroyed that town in minutes! What might two hundred do?" Gerain was aghast.

"That was what worried my parents," said Maria. "That's why I had to marry Ferrian." She suddenly lost all colour. Her hands began to shake. "They'll follow us to Soprafini, won't they? They'll turn the Fireflies loose in the countryside and they'll multiply, there will be thousands of them, more every minute—"

"Stop it!" Philippa shook her shoulders. "It won't be like that—"

"What's to stop them?" Maria turned to face her. "They'll burn up all our people, and all the time there will be more of them—"

"We'd better get there first, then, hadn't we?" said Gerain. "We'd better warn the Sopra-finians."

Philippa looked at him. "It all comes down to the Fireflies, then, doesn't it?"

"The Fireflies and the arethusans," said Gerain.

CHAPTER 21

They knew they would be followed, but for almost a week they travelled with no signs of pursuit. The arethusans towed them swiftly through a lonely countryside, full of woods and moorland. It was well into autumn now, and the days were rapidly shortening. The nights were getting very cold and they huddled together under the upturned boat.

The arethusans made no effort to contact them further. They courteously halted when their passengers wanted to and then disappeared until required again. Looking again at the pretty ornament the arethusan had given her, Philippa found herself wondering about them all the time. Were these arethusans shy or embarrassed . . . or simply uninterested?

They passed very few settlements, a group of mud-dwellers in rough huts, and two or three villages of fisherpeople clustering along the banks of the Ere. No one paid them much attention. Winter was on the way and it was a time for hard work. People were busy from daybreak to nightfall, gathering crops and making jams and preserves and salting meat.

They never stopped for long, anyway: the certainty of pursuit was overwhelming, their memory of the Fireflies all too vivid.

Josquin made a rapid recovery. To pass those long days afloat and to keep everyone's mind off the increasing cold, he suggested that they all practise singing, just in case they had the opportunity to perform. There was no need to make money. The arethusans found fish for them every day, and Gerain occasionally managed to trap a rabbit. There were berries and nuts in abundance everywhere, as well as the occasional outcrop of wild rice. It was not luxurious, as Maria sourly remarked, but at least there was enough.

Philippa observed her former mistress thoughtfully. She had never thought Maria a fool, but this about-turn in character was more than superficial. Philippa had expected the habits of Maria's lifetime to be harder to shift.

And then she wondered at herself, as well. After all, she too had lived in luxury and ease, even if she had been enslaved. It was amazing that they should both have adapted so well to this life of casual vagrancy.

The companionship of Josquin and Gerain had much to do with it. They fell into a pattern of easy conversation. The singing practices were fun for everyone, even though Philippa's voice was virtually inaudible and Gerain's sense of rhythm was at best eccentric. At other times they told stories to each other to pass the time. The water-meadows and mud-flats passed in a dream. Josquin's stories were always outrageous, even in the early days when it was clear that his shoulder still hurt. He clowned around, teasing everyone else, singing bawdy songs, telling them scandals and gossip of times on the road, long into the night.

Gerain was much quieter, but his mouth twitched at Josquin's jokes. They shared some memories, for Miracule's troupe had regularly visited Barusi. But Gerain's own stories ranged over different matters, legends concerning arethusans and mermaids and seal-souls and dolphins.

They were sitting by the riverside one evening. The arethusans had presented them with a catch of fresh-water prawns, before gracefully disappearing off into the depths.

Gerain leaned back against a tree trunk. "Some say that arethusans are the only real mermaids," he said, and Philippa held her breath. "And it is true that when they reach the sea, they have the option of staying underwater or becoming human. That is the choice, the great choice. They can choose to remain in the lands of the deep or to walk on earth. If they do take the human option, they lose their body hair, and the webbing between their fingers becomes more fragile. They become almost entirely human."

"I heard something about that once," said Josquin. "The Lady Aqurelt's a candidate, if ever there was one."

"Didn't you ever ask her?" Maria said.

"It always seemed like – an intrusion. Something private."

"She is a mermaid then!" said Philippa, her eyes bright. "I knew it!"

"More properly, an arethusan, by birth. She'll never admit it," said Gerain. "And on land you see no signs of it, of course, except for those amazing green eyes—"

"But she knows all sorts of things!" said Philippa. "And she's not Barusi, is she? I always thought there was something – exotic about her. . ."

"Well, it's one theory." Josquin pulled her hair gently. "And as for exotic, I would have thought you knew something about that."

"Me? What do you mean?"

"Well, all this clairvoyance, these dreams and pictures in water. Not everyone can do those things, you know."

"Not even all the Barusi," said Gerain. "It's fairly rare, even amongst them. Some say that it's all to do with the arethusans which occasionally stay and become human and intermarry . . . You've probably got arethusan blood somewhere far back, Pip . . . You've even got the green eyes to go with it—"

"What?" She thought she must have misheard him.

"Well, look at your hands. They were webbed once, weren't they? You're at least part arethusan."

"That arethusan at Lowenbridge gave you that clasp, didn't he? He must have recognized you." Maria looked interested. She picked up Philippa's hand and compared it with her own. "My hand's smaller, even though I'm taller than you," she said. "You'd probably be a really good swimmer, if ever you'd learned how to do it."

"So there's this connection between arethusans and aquemancers," said Gerain. "That's one theory, anyway. But very few can see the

262

future. Most aquemancers only reflect what's happening now."

"I – don't really like doing it," Philippa said, her mind racing round the implications of Gerain's words. An *arethusan* for a great-grandma? It was bizarre, but not at all upsetting. She rather liked the idea. . . .

"Rather uncomfortable, I would have thought," Gerain was saying. "Seeing the future, I mean."

She smiled at him. "Too right," she said. "I haven't tried it since we left the inn."

"Now that was what I would call useful," Gerain said. "To warn us like that. An ability worth a very great deal."

"Try it again now," said Josquin. "See what's ahead."

"I don't want to!" She felt suddenly panicky. They were too close, nearly there . . . "Not now. It's not a game."

"I quite agree. This is serious. I think it would be extremely useful to know how close behind the Rustrians are. Whether they're following us at all."

"I can't do it to order!" said Philippa desperately.

"Yes, you can," said Maria. "Just dip your hands overboard—" And as she spoke the arethusans stopped swimming and the skiff drifted to a halt in a clump of reeds.

Hating the pressure of their eyes on her, Philippa leant over the side and scooped up a handful of water.

She saw something almost immediately. Clear and vivid as daylight, a man's face glared at her. His mouth moved and she understood the silent words.

"We're coming," said Marco.

Marco stood among the ruins of the town by the river. The Fireflies were back in their cages, sated and somnolent. The pathetic townspeople still huddled together in the square. Thanks to Philippa's warnings, there were very few children left in the village, and they had all been accounted for. Of the adults, only those who had been wise enough to remain close to water or in the square had remained unharmed. Many others had been caught in the cross-fire and were receiving such medical attention as was available.

Marco surveyed the damage and his eyes were completely expressionless.

At his side, Ferrian was on horseback. He was furious. "We missed them! How is it possible, how did they get away?"

"They had warning."

"How? Who warned them? We were so careful not to alarm them! No riders went between

Lowenbridge and our camp, our soldiers made no attempt to harass them. There was no reason for them to suspect that we were so close—"

"It's that little maid servant. Peering into water, like the conscientious little aquemancer she is. I saw her, you know." Marco looked thoughtful. "She's very unguarded. She doesn't really know what she's doing. Every time she looks into a pool of water, she calls to me."

"What use is that, when we keep missing them?" Ferrian looked ready to order executions. His bulbous eyes were staring around him, as if he might find the fugitives lurking behind the burned-out shells of houses around them.

He leaned forward across the pommel. "Listen to me, Marco of Barusi," he said, very quietly. "Unless you deliver that evil little slut to me very soon, I shall take great delight in feeding you to the Fireflies myself."

Marco stared back at him, unblinking. "They'll probably go south, sire." He pointed to a distant range of mountains. "It's been the pattern so far. I think they're making for the lake."

"For the dam, do you mean?" Ferrian was thoughtful. "But you can't tell for sure, can you?" He sat up straight once more, drumming his fingers against the pommel. "My pyromancers recommend west, you know. Through the mountains, into Soprafini that way."

"Sire, it makes no sense! They'll stick to the river, I'm sure they will—"

"I don't trust you, Marco. I think you're saying this to divert me." He paused for a moment, thinking. Then Ferrian nodded once to himself, as if some decision had been made. He turned to his lieutenant. "Return to Rienzi," he instructed. "Give this to my father . . ." and he took off his gauntlet, "and tell him to send the other Fireflies. All of them." The lieutenant sketched a salute and ran to his horse.

He turned back to Marco. "You have until the Fireflies get here. If you haven't found our fugitives by then, you will salute their arrival with your own flesh." Ferrian looked at Marco. "I've been lenient for too long," he said.

"Sire, your power is as a lightning storm. Certainly, your name will be remembered while men still live." Marco had gone very white.

Ferrian nodded, again. "Tell everyone to unload. We're staying here, just for a while. Until Marco's found our runaways."

CHAPTER 22

Gerain and Philippa sat on a rock next to the river and watched the arethusans far out in the river. They were curving round each other in a sensuous and elaborate dance, flowing together and then breaking away as the currents swept them along.

The arethusans became aware of their audience. Two pairs of liquid green eyes turned towards them and flashed with something like amusement. Then, politely and firmly they dived deeply and Philippa and Gerain knew that they had intruded on some delicate moment of privacy.

Philippa became aware of Gerain's hand on her wrist.

She looked at him quickly. He held his finger to his mouth; shusssh. And in that quiet space of time she thought she almost understood the arethusans' silence, almost understood what it meant.

They knew each other, and they knew her. Their communication was deeper and more subtle than sound and she was within a hair's breadth of understanding it.

"They *must* not die," she said. "It would be like killing – ourselves." She knew this to be true. "We have to help them."

"That's what I think." He leaned forward and kissed her once, gently, on the lips. "I'm glad you understand."

It was a small act, a gesture towards something deeper than companionship. Philippa felt a smile flickering close to the surface.

Gerain sighed, as if awakening. "Josquin says that this canyon passage leads to the lake." He pointed to the walls of rock which were beginning to close around them. "We'll be running fast tomorrow."

She slept that night near the river, where the arethusans lazily drifted in the warm currents, and dreamed of belonging somewhere, of coming home.

Next day it began to rain. The walls of the canyon

rose high above them and it seemed like the sky was funnelling all its water, every drop of moisture into the narrow gap over the gorge, battering down on their heads. In minutes, they were completely soaked.

It was no better in the skiff. The river was indeed running very fast and there were rocks everywhere. Somehow, they were going to have to negotiate a long series of rapids.

And then the arethusans disconnected themselves from the skiff, and briefly looked at the travellers, their faces unreadable. Then they dived into the river, and disappeared back the way they had come.

"Where are they going?" asked Philippa, aghast. "Are they *leaving* us here?"

"We're getting close to the lake," said Gerain. "They never go there, remember? It must mean that we're nearly there."

They could all see that the boat would be useless against such irregular and wild currents without the arethusans. They abandoned the little skiff with some regret and set off on foot, picking their way along the various strata that bordered the river.

It was hard going, complicated by the torrential rain drenching their hair and clothes, distorting their vision. The rock dust beneath their feet turned to slippery mud which clung to their boots. Every step was a major effort.

For two days, they waded through mud and rain. Sometimes there were wide paths alongside the river, but more often they had to balance along narrow ledges. Fortunately, the cliff was fractured by caves and overhangs, and they managed to sleep each night out of the rain. But they were all soaked to the skin and bitterly cold, and there was no wood to build fires.

They had very little food left. They were exhausted. However a sense of urgency gripped them all, especially Maria. It was always she who proposed that they start again after each snatched break. But without the arethusans they were making slow progress. They knew that the Rustrians were on their tail, that there was nowhere safe for them until they reached Soprafini. And that Soprafini itself would be under attack from the most dangerous weapons conceivable.

The river ran like a wild creature beside them, foaming and frothing, swollen by the weight of water falling from the skies.

"At least the Fireflies won't be out," said Josquin. "Not in all this rain."

"They can travel, though. Their cages are water-proof. And when the sun comes out —" Maria made a face.

"We'll be safe and sound the other side of Lake Ere."

"Not necessarily. Why are you always so bright and jolly?"

"It's the pleasure of your company, my poor drowned rat." He was laughing at her, she thought. How can he laugh, when it's all so desperate? But curiously, Maria didn't mind being described as a drowned rat. Looking around them all, she thought it was nothing less than justice. Their hair was plastered to their faces, their cloaks hanging like ragged tails, trailing in the mud.

That same afternoon, just as they were all at the end of their endurance, tired, hungry and cold, Josquin rounded a bend in the rock wall, and stopped dead.

"My God. Now what?" He spoke slowly and softly only to Gerain. The girls were some way behind.

Ahead of them the river opened out, widening into a seamless expanse of still water. Their path now ran around the east rim of Lake Ere. Between two jagged peaks, in the very far distance, they could just see the flat line on the horizon which was the dam.

This was the Lake of Ere, artificially formed, bulging in the west in a vast sweep into the Soprafinian mountains. The far end, distant, only just discernible, was the only way through to Soprafini territory. The road across the dam was guarded by fences and soldiers and barriers, Maria had told them. For although the dam was a symbol of the union between the Rustrians and the Soprafini, both sides insisted on policing the border.

For a moment Josquin and Gerain stood in silence under an overhang, gazing at the tideless grey sea, the rain sheeting in great swathes over its surface.

"It depends how well the dam is guarded," said Gerain, at last. "And whether we can convince the Soprafinians. . . ."

"We've got to get there first," Josquin said. "We're on the Rustrian side here. It's the most direct, the quickest way to the dam. But we'll also be most vulnerable to the Rustrian army."

"It's still raining," said Gerain. "The Fireflies won't be out. We'll be all right."

But even as he spoke, the clouds in the east rolled back and a small patch of blue suddenly broke through the banks of grey.

A wind blew up, tossing the heavy clouds aside and then the rain stopped and the blue spread and grew and filled all the sky.

The sun came out as the girls caught up with them.

"So much for the Fireflies," said Josquin. "It's

lunacy to stay on this side."

"We're too *slow* to chance the long way round," said Maria. Philippa looked from one to the other. "The Rustrians will beat us to the dam, they'll be into Soprafini long before we get there. We *have* to get there first."

"Come on, we don't even know for sure that they're still following us." Gerain leant against a rock and scraped his boots one against the other. Clods of mud fell on the ground. There was no sound at all from the mountains, no rustle of wind or birdsong.

"Well, what do you think?" Josquin looked at him. "What do you think the Rustrians were doing at that town by the river? They were looking for us. For Maria."

"We've seen nothing of them since."

"For which we must be thankful. But I think we have to assume that we're still being followed. I vote we go round the long way. I am not in the least anxious to meet Fireflies again. Are you?"

They were all tired, hungry and irritable. Gerain stared at him. "You didn't have to come. Why don't you go back and find Miracule and all the rest of your nice friendly family? If you're so frightened?"

For the first time since they'd known him, Josquin looked impatient. "Listen. We either cross the river and take the safe, long way round, on the Soprafinian side of the lake, and get to the pass – oh, sometime next week, I reckon. Some days, at any rate. Or we stay on this side and chance the Rustrians and the Fire-flies, and follow the short route. I'm not frightened, not much, but we have to make a reasoned decision *now,* at this point. Don't we?"

"All right," Gerain conceded. "You're right, as usual." He turned to Philippa. "What do you think we should do?"

Philippa looked blank. "How can I tell?"

"Try some of this famous aquemancy. Tell our fortunes," suggested Josquin.

Maria looked frantic. "Must we waste time? We *have* to get there first! The short route is the only route! There's no point in any of this if the Rustrians get into Soprafini—"

"Let Philippa try," said Gerain. "It won't take long, will it, Pip?"

"Must I?" She was always so reluctant, so frightened of what she might find. Marco, hands of bone . . . that child. . . .

"Oh, go on, Philippa. Don't fuss. If it gets us closer to a decision, it'll be worth it," said Maria.

Gerain put his arm round her shoulder. "It's now or never, Philippa," he said seriously. "This is the final leg, the end of it. We have to know what to do."

"We're here now, anyway." She spoke softly and they saw her move to the edge of the path. She stood there for a moment looking out over the lake. The cold wind rustled through her short hair, whipping at the folds of her cloak. It was very quiet. Her eyes were wide and staring.

There were tears in them, brought by no wind. "Oh, no," she whispered. "Not here, not now—"

"What do you mean?" Maria had her by the shoulders. "What are you talking about?"

Philippa stared at the lake as if it were made of tears. Grey water reflected in her eyes. "Oh, it's so sad! So terrible, poor child, poor little girl. . . ."

"What? What are you talking about?" Maria asked sharply.

"Look at the water, can't you see her?" Her hands moved slowly, widening towards the entirety of the lake. "She's deep now, very deep down. So lonely, she is . . . How evil, how dreadful . . ." She grasped Maria's arm. "Look there, Maria, over there!"

"There's nothing there! What are you talking about?" Maria was shouting at her, infuriated by Philippa's mysterious words. All she could see, all Josquin and Gerain could see was the flat expanse of grey water, waiting silently beneath the shadow of the mountains.

"And it's all going to drain away," Philippa said at last, "and then we'll find her. Maria, you'll find her. All this water . . . I've seen it, it's true. It's going to happen."

"Find *who?*" Maria was furious.

Philippa shook her head suddenly, as if emerging from water. Her eyes had cleared. "I don't know," she said mournfully. "I don't know who she is, I don't know what she's doing there in the lake, she's just a baby! I don't understand any of it!"

"This is no use." Gerain looked from one to the other of them. "We have to decide about which route to take. No one understands whatever it is you're seeing, Philippa, it makes no sense. But it does make sense to get to Soprafini as fast as we can. Otherwise they'll overtake us. Don't you agree?"

Maria straightened her shoulders. "Come on," she said. "Use your eyes. It's obvious. We'll have to stay on this Rustrian side anyway. We'll never get across without arethusans."

"You're right, of course." Josquin looked behind them at the frantic torrent, forward to the wide, distant shore. There was no bridge, no ford or crossing point. He sighed. "Let's try to outrun them. Are you ready, Philippa?"

"I hate this place," she said softly. "It's like death, being here."

But still she pulled her cloak more closely round her and followed the others along the narrow lakeside path.

CHAPTER 23

Marco had been watching. "Well, who'd have thought it?" he said softly.

The Rustrian pyromancers stared at him with dislike.

"Have you found them?" asked Tracho, Ferrian's personal chief of pyromancy. He was furious that this Barusi barbarian should be more adept than he.

They were assembled in a pavilion erected at Ferrian's command. Guards stood just inside the entrance, in case Marco should try anything. The pyromancers had assembled their great glass trays, scattered with patterns of ash. They tilted them this way and that, looking for significance in the way the ash fell.

Marco used only a bowl of water.

"Call the prince," he said to the Rustrian guard who attended all sessions of aquemancy. "We've found them."

Ferrian arrived minutes later, his sharp eyes glowing with anticipation.

"Far from here?" he asked. "Are they far away?"

"No, not far. Not far at all. And that silly little girlie is meddling yet again, sending out flags and flares through the water. Really, they may as well be announcing it in bright lights from the top of the Rignal Mountains."

"Where *precisely*?" Ferrian's fist slammed down on the table. The water in Marco's bowl splashed and spilled on to the floor.

Marco was aware of danger. He recalled himself.

"Sire, they've reached the lake," he said formally. "They're on the east shore, just the other side of the ridge from the highway. They're going to chance outrunning us by sticking close to the lake."

"We'll catch them, then," said Ferrian.

"And the rain's stopped," said Tracho, who had been watching all this. "What about sending the Fireflies on ahead to meet them?"

"Now, that is an interesting idea." Ferrian showed his sharp teeth for a moment. "But I do like to see my darlings in action. It would be rather a waste. I know," he said happily. "We'll all go."

They thought they would be safe while they kept close to the lake. Their path was too narrow, too irregular for the carts and heavy artillery of the Rustrian army. They were moving quickly, too, clambering over the frequent rockfalls, helping each other over the muddy chasms, the difficult ledges. Philippa and Gerain were invaluable, somehow managing to cling to the rock, always finding safe hand and footholds when the path disappeared altogether, as it did rather too often.

They did not dare to rest. They knew that the Soprafinian border was very close. They made good time, but they were still no more than half way to the dam when the Rustrian army drew level with them.

The first they knew of it was the smell of burning on the air.

Maria recognized it at once. She stopped suddenly, holding out her hand to halt the others. "Oh, no . . ." she said, her nose wrinkled. "Can you smell it? Scorching, burning. . . ."

And beyond the fresh scent of water and mud, something sour and acrid wafted towards them.

"It's no forest fire, that's for sure," said Josquin. He frowned. "What now?"

And then they heard its noise, the dreadful roaring of the furnace, up ahead. They didn't wait to see what it was, they knew. As one they turned and ran back along the path they'd just travelled.

But the smell of burning did not decrease and the roaring came louder, in front of them now.

A bright flaming light, brighter and more sudden than lightning dazzled them. And there was a Firefly hurtling towards them, fizzing and hissing over the damp rock. Behind them, another closed in.

They saw the briefest of impressions, of red eyes, spiny limbs and sparking breath in one tiny, terrified instant.

"The lake!" shouted Josquin. "Now!"

There was literally no alternative.

From the top of the cliff, Prince Ferrian, Marco and the Rustrian pyromancers watched the fugitives dive straight into the lake below them, straight into the calm sheet of water.

Ferrian saw four dark heads resurface and that two of them were in immediate difficulties. "They can't even swim," he said, amused. "Now what?"

He saw the other two grab hold of the non-swimmers and start towing them out into the centre of the lake, making for the middle of the dam.

Ferrian smiled at Marco. "We'll pick them up as we cross over, shall we? On the way to Sopra-fini."

He gave a series of orders and the Fireflies were restrained once more in their watery cages. Then the Rustrian army, complete with all its soldiers and equipment and strange machines and monsters, continued along the top of the cliff towards the dam.

Below them, four small dark heads bobbed in the lake.

"Look, what's going on over there?" The Soprafinian soldier tried to shade his eyes against the sun-reflecting water. He was standing midway along the dam, looking out over the lake. "Sir, there are people swimming there!"

"Better put a boat out," the Captain sighed. Very occasionally there were refugees from the Rustrian side. Sometimes, the bedraggled swimmers were escaped criminals or dissidents. There was always paperwork involved, endless enquiries and trouble, whatever the case.

But the prospect of increased paperwork soon vanished from the Captain's mind. As they rowed out towards the four swimmers, he found himself idly scanning the far side of the bank, and saw the gleam of metal.

His oars dropped from his hands. His companion glanced at him, and then turned to look too.

The little boat stopped moving, hanging there over the depths as the two Soprafinian soldiers faced the appalling realization that the entire Rustrian army was slowly moving towards them along the east road, making for the dam.

"They're attacking!" said the soldier breathlessly. "My God, what have they got in those cages?"

The Captain pulled himself together. With a cool eye, he measured distances. He said, "Quickly, gather up these fools. Perhaps they know what's going on."

And so they hauled the four disreputable-looking young people into their boat and listened in disbelief as one of them, a woman dressed in man's clothes, announced herself as the Princess Maria of Soprafini.

The soldiers had wanted information, but this was ridiculous. The one thing the Captain remembered about the Princess was the great mass of blonde hair twined into an elaborate knot with cascading curls. This ragamuffin bore no relation to the elegant young lady from Caer Corelli.

Anyway, they had an emergency facing them. Back on the dam, they threw the four young people into a cell attached to the guardhouse and locked the door securely.

Then the Captain sent the soldier with a frantic message to the nearby barracks.

For a while he watched the progress of the Rustrians towards the dam. It would take them an hour, he reckoned, before they were in a position to cross. It would take the men from the barracks about the same time to get themselves here.

Too long. And too few. There were only a hundred men in the barracks; there was no chance of seriously resisting a large-scale attack from Rustria. No one in Soprafini had expected an invasion, especially with the marriage treaty now finalized.

What had happened? Why were they attacking *now,* now that the marriage had been solemnized? He frowned. That girl . . . *was* she the princess? Was she telling the truth? For a moment he stood on the dam, undecided. There was nothing he could do on his own to hold back the Rustrians. He might as well find out what he could.

And so he went to question his prisoners further.

*   *   *

It was possible. Yet again, he cast his mind back to that windy night, when he'd helped the princess from her coach and into the Rustrian. Her hair was unrecognizable, but she'd explained that. It could be, it could just be. . . .

"Very well, let's accept, just for the sake of argument that you are indeed the Princess Maria. How does Your Highness explain your current situation? We were told that the marriage with Prince Ferrian was to have been solemnized some weeks ago. Why are you here?"

He was sitting in a chair tilted against the desk on the other side of the bars. He looked casual and at ease, but half his mind was fretting over the position of those Rustrian troops. They'll be over the ridge, he kept thinking. They'll be halfway down the bluff. . . .

The two young men were standing by the bars, the smaller girl was lying on the bunk. They were all shivering with cold.

The blonde one, the one who called herself Maria Soprafini, was glaring at him. She drew herself up. "On the eve of my marriage to Prince Ferrian I discovered that the Rustrians were going to attack Soprafini. That the marriage treaty was just a ploy to lure my father into a false sense of security. I escaped, with my maid, here, and these kind friends. The Rustrians are about to invade Soprafini! We have to find some way to defend ourselves!"

I know that! the Captain said to himself impatiently. *Was* she telling the truth?

"Look!" she said, thrusting her hand through the bars. The great sapphire ring of Soprafini glared balefully at him. "Why don't you believe me?"

"And this is your – maid, did you say?" The Captain looked at Philippa, lying on the narrow bed by the wall.

She groaned. She had said not a word, since falling into the lake. The great wrong which she had envisioned beneath its surface had gripped her with a physical force. She felt ill, as if she had touched evil, as if she were tainted.

"Philippa! Come on, tell the Captain who you are!" Maria snapped at her. This was too urgent for kind and gentle words.

Philippa rolled over, and Gerain helped her into a sitting position. "You have to drain the water," she said simply. "Breach the dam and drain the lake—"

The Captain stared at her as if she were mad. And yet the small voice at the back of his mind suddenly leapt with exultation. "Breach the dam?" he shouted. "What treason is this?"

Maria exchanged glances with Josquin. "No

treason. No treason at all. It might just save the day. . . ."

He stared at her, the idea beginning to gather force.

"I could not possibly give such orders! The responsibility—"

"Is mine." Maria looked at him coldly. "I will answer to my father. And the prize, holding back the Rustrian army, will give us time to defend ourselves. You will be a great hero, Captain. Your name will echo down the centuries."

"If only we could get authorization! There's no time—" His face was agonized.

"Captain." Maria spoke softly. "Do you believe I am who I say I am?"

For answer, he stood up and released the doors to the prison. He had made up his mind. Slowly, he nodded. "You carry the ring. You are used to wielding power. None but the royal family would have the audacity, the courage to propose such a scheme."

"Very well then. Tell us what to do."

The Captain became very busy.

"What do you know about engineering?" he said, as they went back out into the open. "There are sluice gates, the overflow, various safeguards. . . ."

"Surely it's not that difficult? If we shut the

sluice gates, and the overflow, then the dam will be under pressure, won't it?" Josquin sounded confident.

"Wait until they're half way across," said Maria, inspired. "Until they've got the Fireflies out . . . If we time it right, we could drown the Fireflies too!"

They looked at each other, the plan now complete, instantly, brilliantly. "Yes! Come on," said Josquin. "Show us. What should we do?"

"Very well." The Captain gave instructions as they all left the guardhouse.

Across the dam, they could see the bright colours, the blue and silver of the Rustrian army spreading like glossy litter over the dull rocks. They were very close to the other end of the dam.

Next to the guardhouse stood the control hut. There were levers there and a great wheel. The Captain pointed out the various controls, the way the pressure was finely balanced. Without delay they set to, turning the wheel as far as it would go, opening all the levers to their fullest extent.

"Will it be enough?" asked Gerain. "How do we know the dam will go if we do all this?"

The Captain, a tall, sandy-haired man with worried eyes, frowned. "We don't. There's been a lot of rain, the lake's as high as I've ever seen it. The pressure is high right now, but—" He stopped. They could see it in his face.

He didn't know if it would be enough. No one did.

"We'll need something more," said Philippa grimly. "It's been built to withstand this kind of pressure. We need something else. . . ."

"We need geomancers!" said Gerain savagely. "A trained Barusi geomancer could do it without thinking, set off an avalanche or something. There are enough rocks around, surely—"

In the sudden silence everyone except the Captain turned to Philippa. "Could you do it, Pip?" Maria said, taking her hand. "You and Gerain, between you. If we got you up on the cliff, could you set it off—?"

Philippa looked astounded. "I've never done anything like that before! I don't know, I wouldn't know where to begin—"

"It wouldn't need much," said the Captain slowly. "The cliff at the back there is very precipitous. And years ago, when we started building the dam, and the Barusi tried to stop us, there was a lot of trouble up there. They were trying to set off an avalanche then . . . We caught the ringleaders before any damage was done, but the rubble is still all in place. We had to shore it up behind a boulder, to make sure. We could probably do it manually, but it's difficult to get to—"

"Which cliff?" asked Gerain, looking at the blank rock all around them.

"There," said the Captain, pointing at the sheer grey wall just behind the guardhouse. "A fall from there would destroy the dam. Probably. But we'd need specialist climbers for it. It's impossible."

Gerain and Philippa looked at the rock face, the minute threads of cracks that ran over its surface. Philippa swallowed. Just big enough for her fingers, she reckoned, although she didn't know how Gerain would manage.

"Very well." She looked at him. "Shall we give it a try?"

CHAPTER 24

Prince Ferrian, his more favoured officers and his most highly regarded pyromancers reached the side of the dam. They conferred with the officers in the Rustrian checkpoint there, and made an assessment of the Soprafinians' actions.

They had all seen the level of the lake rise. They knew that the Soprafinians would be attempting to breach the dam, to delay the Rustrian invasion. It amused them, nothing more. They looked at the great sweep of the dam's wall and were still supremely confident.

"The dam won't go because a few gates have been shut off," said Ferrian disdainfully. "Not for hours. We'll get across well before that."

"All of us?" Marco regarded the ranks of soldiers, the great carts with their cannons and the Firefly cages.

Ferrian shrugged. "Possibly there might be a few stragglers who get their feet wet. . . ."

"Sire," Tracho was trembling with anxiety. "Even if we do get over, if the dam goes we'll have no way back!"

"We won't need it." Ferrian smiled at him. "So long as we and the Fireflies are on the other side, the Soprafinians have not one chance. Not a snowball's hope in hell."

"An appropriate metaphor, Your Highness," Marco bowed.

"But I wouldn't like to risk the Fireflies getting wet," continued Ferrian thoughtfully. "They will be at the head of the army. I and my personal guard will lead the way, and they will be just behind. We'll get over there long before anyone from Soprafini has the wit to stop us."

"They're sending a rider to the barracks now, sire," said one of the lookouts.

Ferrian was unconcerned. "A reception committee. How delightful."

He put on his favourite white velvet cloak with its ruby red lining and gold clasps. He allowed his Master of Horses to hand him up on to his great grey stallion. And then, at the head of the long procession of Firefly carts, he started the long ride out into the middle of the dam.

At least it wasn't raining, Philippa told herself, clinging to the rocks above the guardhouse. Gerain was a little way along from her. He looked at her, flashing a quick grin. "How are you doing?" he asked.

"Fine." She had no breath for anything else. Trouble was, she wasn't fine, not at all. The wind that gusted through the valley was sharp and bitter with cold. She was shivering all the time, her fingers almost numb. If it got any worse, she would just drop to the ground, like rotten fruit from a tree.

She looked down to see where the ground was and immediately regretted it. Maria and Josquin looked like dolls, the Captain nothing more than a toy soldier. And behind her, on the other side of the lake, were a thousand other soldiers, ten times that number, on their way to overwhelm and overrun the dam.

"Come on," said Gerain. He was above her now, almost at the point which they'd decided looked likely.

She leaned her head against the rock-face, breathing on her cramped fingers, trying to warm them a little. Then she took a deep breath, and stretched upwards for the next handhold.

On the ground, Maria said to Josquin, quietly, "If it works, we could win it all."

Like her, his face was angled upwards towards Philippa and Gerain, high above them. He watched their slow movements without comment. "It's all a question of timing," he said.

It was so crucial. A few minutes early and the Rustrians would be merely delayed on their side of the border. A few minutes late and they would all be across.

This was supposing they could break the dam at all. It might prove impossible. Looking at that great solid wall, thickening towards its base, Maria knew that it would take vast forces. But they would need more than force: to get the timing right, they would also need luck. In less than an hour, the Fireflies could be running loose in Soprafini.

Maria could hardly bear to contemplate it. She frowned. "It's got to work. This is my responsibility. This is all my fault."

Josquin looked at her then. Nearly as tall as he, slim and graceful. Her face was more interesting than beautiful, the mouth perhaps too wide, the nose too strong. But the fine hair was pale as straw, delicately framing her face and the colour of her eyes took his breath away.

"If this goes through, we may never meet again." He spoke slowly. "You'll return to court life, and marry some noble. Lassan, or someone. I'll never see you again."

She could say nothing.

"But, if this works, if it happens as we hope, I want you to know . . . I really . . . I've really loved getting to know you, Maria. I'll never forget these last few weeks." He raised his hand gently and stroked her cheek. "Streets above any spoilt princess . . . I'd cross oceans for you, if you wanted." A quick grin. "With or without arethusans."

For a moment, she held his hand between hers. "Always the showman, Jos . . . But I believe you." A pause as she looked out again across the waters of the lake. "I'd give anything not to be who I am. I'd give anything to be the girl you sing with, some travelling entertainer in Miracule's troupe . . . But it's no good. There's no way round it."

"I know." He turned away from her. "Let's go and tell our fine Captain that they're nearly there."

For a moment, all three of them watched Philippa and Gerain clinging to the rock-face.

Behind them, the level of the lake was visibly

rising. Soon it would begin to lap the top of the dam.

The Rustrians had seen it too. They were moving at a run, very fast, down the sloping hills towards the dam.

Maria and Josquin looked at the Captain, shading his eyes to see more clearly.

"How long have we got?" Maria asked him.

He wiped his hand across his sweating brow. "My lady, without a fall of rocks, the dam's not going to go. Water pressure alone is certainly not going to be enough. This is the most ambitious piece of engineering in Soprafini. It may be more secure than we think."

"Never before have I wished for incompetent workmanship . . ." Maria mused.

"If this comes off—" He stared at her. "I'll either be court-martialled or given a medal."

"You're only obeying orders." She wished that she had that particular let-out. She couldn't begin to think what her parents would say.

Scenarios flashed through her mind. Her father nodding, satisfied, his hand on her shoulder. Her mother, "Darling! You saved us all—" A scented embrace, kisses, approval at last.

She couldn't imagine it. They were too formal, too cold. Another glance at the two tiny figures struggling high above them and then Maria leaned against the railing, looking down into the inky dark waters lapping softly far beneath her.

Water, shifting . . . "What was here before?" she asked the Captain softly. "Before the dam was built?"

He shrugged. "The locals have it that there's a grave there. Some nameless person's grave. They say it's cursed, that whoever it is won't rest."

"Won't rest? Do you mean . . . . ghosts?"

He paused for a moment before answering. "No . . . at least, it could have been just a trick of the light."

"What?" She turned round, leaning against the rail and regarded him. "What do you mean, a trick of the light?"

He flushed again under her gaze. He was embarrassed. She felt more than a little sympathetic towards him. "Every now and then . . . on the midnight watch, people see shapes in the water. Curving shapes, something that gleams and shines, like bone. . . ."

"Have you seen this?"

He nodded. She turned back to the water, but all she could see was her own face, a pale moon-shape reflected in the dark depths.

The soldier's story reminded her of Philippa's visions.

Whose bones lay beneath the lake? Why

could they not rest there, why were they not quiet?

Philippa would find out, when the waters were drained away. Philippa, who was at least half an aquemancer, still clinging to the cliff high above them.

A metre from the top, she almost fell. The ledge she'd hooked her fingers round suddenly crumbled and for one terrible instant her hand scrabbled and scraped against the cliff before her fingers caught and held in another crack.

Blood drained down her arm.

She was tired as death, cold as the tomb.

"Philippa!" Real anxiety in Gerain's voice. She made a final wrenching effort and flopped over on to the ledge next to Gerain. For a moment they clung together, breathing hard. Then Philippa sat back on her heels, wiping the blood from her hand against her breeches. "Come on," she said briskly. "Let's see what we can do."

At the end of the ledge a tumble of rocks was shored up behind one big boulder, set deep in the cliff. "That's it," said Gerain. "That's what's got to go."

They stared at it in growing dismay. The rock jutted from the cliff face, solid, immensely heavy, immovable. It was part of the cliff itself, part of a mountain.

It was impossible to think of it shifting.

They scrambled over it, they bent double to look underneath it and nowhere was there a crack or any other sign of weakness. To push rocks round it or behind it would be too slow, a waste of time and effort.

"Over to you," said Gerain. He squeezed her hand encouragingly.

Below them, the lake was swollen, full of heaving grey water. It made Philippa feel sick to look at it.

She laid her hand on the rock and closed her eyes.

"Aren't you going to sing?" said Gerain. He sounded puzzled. "That's what Barusi geomancers do."

"You've heard me sing. You don't seriously imagine such a feeble sound would make any impression against this, do you?"

He sighed. "Sorry. But I don't understand—"

"Just give me a moment, Gerain. Please."

Her hand on the rock once more, feeling the cold, damp surface and concentrating, concentrating so hard. There was no response, nothing at all. When she'd looked into water, even when it hadn't worked, she'd seen the sky or her face. Water reflected, it moved, it was responsive.

Stone was just itself. Dull and grey, gritty and

grainy under her touch, locking all its secrets away, hard and fast.

Beyond her reach. She did not know how to touch something so blank, so ancient, so dead. No way through, nothing. Sighing, she ran her fingers over its wet and slippery surface.

Under her fingers she felt a ridge in the rock, a small and intricate pattern. Her eyes opened. Softly she rubbed away at the accumulation of mud and dust.

The webbed hand there touched her fingers. A shape in the rock, a fossil or a carving, she didn't know which. But a hand with webbed fingers lay beneath her own and she matched finger to finger, palm and wrist together.

A webbed hand, passing high above the water. The vision fitted. This was meant.

The lightest of pushes, nothing more than a nudge, really.

The stone trembled.

Below them, far away, the Rustrians were already right out on the dam, pushing and trundling along the heavy carts of the Fireflies. She saw that the guardhouse was now empty, that the Captain and Maria and Josquin had moved far away from the dam, back down the road to Soprafini.

The stone shivered. Her hand was cold, and blood still ran from her fingers. *Please, please . . .*

now! she cried silently.

And the stone shifted a little, shifted to one side and then again. She kept her hand in place on that other, webbed hand, and pushed, again.

She never knew exactly what happened next. For Gerain suddenly grabbed her shoulders, hauling her back along the ledge, trying desperately to get out of the way of the collapsing cliff. For the shivering rock was part of a mountain, and its shifting disturbed the bones and the muscles of that mountain.

The rock beneath them was moving. There was a great roaring sound from somewhere deep in the earth itself. And, slowly at first, the rock began to fall.

Although Gerain was so close, trying to protect her from the falling stones, she could see, just once more before it was lost forever, the salute of the webbed hand.

The cliff disintegrated around them.

CHAPTER 25

"It's going! It's shifting—" Josquin clutched Maria's hand. "Look there—" And then he stopped.

A gasping cry from Maria.

They were standing on the south side of the pass leading to Soprafini, just above the level of the dam. It was a useful vantage point, pointing northeast. They could see the wide curving wall of the dam with the Fireflies' carts straddled across the top of it. They could see the expanse of the swollen lake beyond, and the cliffs where Gerain and Philippa were perched.

They saw the great boulder judder, saw it rock on its base. They saw it begin to fall, and the deep rift in the cliff suddenly yawn wide. A vast, tumbling chaos of dust and rock and stone and just a dash of colour, of bright, emerald silk. . . .

Philippa's handkerchief, tossing vividly amongst the rocks, falling far down into the lake.

"Philippa!" Maria had started forward.

"Wait!" Josquin wouldn't let her go. "It's not safe!"

"They're – oh, no, no, no!" She was still trying to struggle free.

"There's nothing we can do! Think, Maria!"

He held her and together they watched the cliff face fall, some into the lake, the rest on to the dam itself.

The men on the dam were running, some leaping into the lake, others just falling, their arms over their heads. There was no hope for them. And just beyond them the first cage of Fireflies was immediately crushed, the next two knocked sideways over the edge. And as they fell, screaming all the way, the wall of the dam cracked and shattered.

The noise rocketed around the mountains. A foaming mess of water and stone spewed out into the air over the valley on the far side, just below where Josquin and Maria were standing. There was a frantic rush as the remaining

Rustrians tried to get back to land. But the other bank was crowded with soldiers and there was no room for them.

It all happened too fast, anyway. The breach in the dam had destroyed the entire structure. Maria and Josquin watched appalled as the curving wall disintegrated, crumbling as if it were made of sand. A great wave of water began to cascade into the valley, crashing over the fields and woods that lay there. What had been a stream became a torrent. Trees were pushed over, plucked from the earth, and tossed through the foaming wave like matchsticks.

Maria was crying, tears running down her face.

"Wait here. Don't move." Josquin's face was grim. "Promise me, Maria. Stay here." And then he kissed her briefly and set off at a run. Maria saw him vanish amongst the trees that led into the newly drowned valley.

"Be careful," she whispered and without thinking the words formed. "Oh, my love, be careful. . . ."

She couldn't breathe. There was cold water all around her and no breath in her lungs. This was terrifying, worse than the awful plunge through the air in the middle of all those rocks and stones. Water was her friend! How could she die here, drowned like some useless kitten?

But she couldn't breathe and her lungs hurt and there was a red mist rising before her eyes. The effort was too much, Philippa was too tired and didn't even know which way was up.

Her legs kicked feebly and then stopped. She could hold it no longer. Her mouth opened and cold water flooded into her face, into her lungs, everywhere.

She knew nothing else.

Josquin half slid down the bank, half fell, towards the torrent which now flooded the valley south of the dam. Brambles caught at his feet as he blundered through the branches and undergrowth. All the time he was slipping in the mud from the recent rains. And then his feet skidded out of control, and he tumbled down over the bank. His hand caught a branch just in time and he stopped himself from pitching into the angry waters that now rushed over the floor of the valley.

He didn't know what he would find, whether it was even worth looking. He couldn't begin to imagine how Philippa and Gerain could ever survive that fall into the lake. There had been too many rocks falling with them. But he had to look. He had to try.

What he didn't expect to see was the remains

of one of the Firefly cages. It bobbed up suddenly, quite close to where he was standing. For a moment it was caught in an eddy and twirled . . . And then the cage was gripped by the current and was torn away past him, and all he could see was an impression of something black and slimy spreading itself over the bottom of the cage, something that screamed a dying wail, as it twitched and shivered. He watched as the Firefly's remains dissolved into the surface of the metal, and as the cage disappeared out of sight, he knew that it was no more.

Josquin felt sick. He stood at the side of the torrent clinging to a silver birch, and watched the floating debris, and every now and then he saw someone, saw the head of a Rustrian soldier, or a shoulder or an arm wearing blue and white cloth, Rustrian army colours.

There was no sign of Philippa. No sign of Gerain.

Underwater. A rocking, softening medium, supporting her limbs as easily as driftwood. Slowly, gradually, her eyes opened against sea water. Green met green.

Out of the moving water she saw someone reaching towards her, someone's strange, long-fingered hand opening to take hers. The fingers were webbed. Philippa didn't understand. The arethusan smiled and his hands clasped her lightly, gently to his breast. She felt his heart beat against her, the same rhythm, the same pulse.

Don't be frightened, he said silently in her mind. *This is your heritage, this is your other life. . . .*

He opened his arms and showed her a scene of greys and greens, of subtly moving fishes, of soft waving weeds. She hardly understood what he meant. Around her the water was turbulent, full of strange eddies and currents. She saw whirlpools edged with silver, chains of iridescent bubbles drifting like jewels.

Was she *dead*? Was this a dream?

You are part arethusan, said her companion. *You can stay with us here, in the water. You can swim in the tides, you can dance with the fishes—*

As I do, said someone else and Philippa recognized this presence, recognized the warmth of the welcome.

This was the arethusan who had given her the coral and pearl clasp in her hair. He was idling in the currents, his soft and silky fur waving softly around him. *Come join us here, little one,* he said silently. *It's your birthright, you are one of us, my sister's only child. . . .*

Your sister—?

Aqurelt, seal-soul sister of mine, mother of you—

Aqurelt? Aqurelt is my mother?

He touched the pearl clasp. Magic ran through his fingertips, sparkling, inspiring, transformatory.

She looked at the clasp and the water waving over the shapes of faces and starfish and sea-horses softened the outline, adjusting and changing until a face formed.

Aqurelt's face, shifting all the time as water ran over it. The lines softened and disappeared, the face fined down from old to young and she saw herself, a young girl with Aqurelt's eyes.

My mother . . .? Aqurelt, my mother? I'm an arethusan?

You were stolen from her during the troubles when the dam was built. So much unhappiness, so much grief . . . but you are now found, one of us, our own sea-child returned.

This was incredible, extraordinary. And yet she believed it entirely. While one part of her mind was blank with amazement and joy, another part of her stretched out into the water, luxuriating in the ebb and flow.

It was cool around her, gently lifting her limbs, enticing her into movement, into response . . . Philippa flexed her muscles and moved towards her new companion.

She could swim! Naturally as an otter, her hands knew how to brace themselves against the water. For a moment, distracted, she looked at her fingers, and saw the remnants of webbing growing there . . .

If you choose to stay with us, your hands will become as ours, said her friend, Aqurelt's brother. Her uncle! He smiled at her and she touched her hands to his face. He held in his hands a garland of water weeds.

She almost took it. And remembered Gerain. *My friend!* she cried in the water. *My dear friend, where is he? I have to find him!*

She saw an expression flickering across the arethusan's face, something she didn't understand. Regret was it? or sympathy? Something complicated and affectionate. . . .

Come with me. He took her hand and together they swam through the drowned ruins of trees, the grass that waved like weed, the jumble of rocks and stone from the dam.

In the clouded water they could see drowned bodies everywhere, the ruins of carts and machinery. She paid no attention to them, drifting here and there, looking and searching for the familiar long-limbed body.

They saw the battered shapes of cages, black sludge clinging to the bars. There was nothing recognizable left of the Fireflies, nothing of their speed and fire and fury. They saw dead men floating by with their eyes and mouths open, their gaudy uniforms stained by mud.

At last they found Gerain wedged between two rocks, his eyes closed, his skin white as bone.

He's dead! Philippa felt her tears flowing into the water, as her hands reached out.

No. Not yet. Her mother's brother pulled Gerain loose from the rock and kicked upwards, strongly.

Philippa followed, knowing it was hopeless.

But there, as the sunlight broke through the water, there was Josquin standing on the bank, reaching down to help Gerain out of the water.

He lay there, collapsed, beached like a fish. The arethusan knew what to do. He blew his own breath into Gerain's mouth and compressed his chest and worked hard. Josquin and Philippa did what they could until, at last, after a nightmare period of anxiety, Gerain coughed and spluttered and choked his way back to consciousness.

And then there was a reunion, much hugging and affection, and when it was over and they were all settled together, Philippa looked back to the seething river.

It ran all the way from the canyon now. The level between lake and river had equalized. The River Ere was back on its former course and the ruins of the dam barely checked its flow to the sea. The remnants of the Rustrian army were in disarray on the far side.

Where a lake had stood, the river ran. A wasteland of mud and debris littered its banks. "Maria," said Josquin, following her gaze. "Let's go and find her. She'll be worrying."

Together, wearily, they tramped back up the bank. Only when they reached the top did Philippa remember to look back. She saw the arethusan watching her, his webbed hand raised in farewell.

She matched her hand to his, acknowledging that they were more than friends and turned back to Gerain, wearily sagging against Josquin.

"Come on," she whispered. "It'll be all right now. Not far now. . . ."

Behind her the river was full of silvery, sinuous shapes hurtling to the sea.

The arethusans were going home.

CHAPTER 26

Maria stood on the hills above the broken dam and watched the river run smooth and fast over the valley, where the lake had been. It looked peaceful and calm, but hundreds, possibly thousands had died. All the Fireflies, although that was no loss. A large part of the Rustrian army including Ferrian himself and Marco. . . .

So many deaths. And Soprafini was safe now, safe for the foreseeable future. But she could feel no victory, no sense of triumph. Her parents had arrived the night before and were encamped to the west of the river. They had greeted their daughter with stiff courtesy and some reproach.

"You should never have breached that dam! It was irresponsible and dangerous," her father had said, scowling. "And running away like that! It was dishonourable, the act of a coward. We are shamed by your behaviour."

"You have disappointed us," her mother added coldly.

"But the Rustrians were about to invade," she'd cried, unable to believe what she was hearing.

"If you had stayed for the marriage, all would have been well," said Gregor severely. "The Rustrians would not have dreamed of attacking—"

"But Prince Ferrian was determined—"

"Do not answer back!" He was very angry. "And now, because of the ludicrous acts of you and your friends, our line of defence, our great lake has been drained!" He exchanged looks with his wife. She was very pale, her hands clasped together.

"You should never have done it," Olivia said. "That lake should have been left undisturbed."

They were implacable.

Maria had run from their presence in a flood of tears. She had never felt close to them, although she had always been in awe of them. But to have them turn against her *now*, when everything she'd done had been in order to save Soprafini!

She found Philippa waiting outside and

together the two walked away from the royal encampment, towards the drained valley.

"I just don't understand!" said Maria. "It was almost as if they were more upset about the draining of the lake than anything else!"

And then they stood staring at each other, each remembering in the same instant that original vision of Philippa's.

The waters draining away and bones there, curving and white. . . .

"Come on," said Philippa abruptly. "Let's go and see."

It was morning, and the sun was bright and clear. They picked their way through the pass back to the ruins of the dam. They saw beneath them the scene set by Philippa's vision, the scene she'd described so very often.

And although Maria now knew that the waters did indeed take death with them, she did not understand how they could leave death behind them.

It was very quiet. Somewhere she heard a bird sing, a blackbird was it? And then something glimmered, something caught in the midday sunlight and gleamed from the valley floor. A curve of bone, like a skeleton hand, beckoning to her, calling her.

"Will you come with me?" she asked Philippa softly. "This is due to you, after all. . . ."

For a moment Philippa hesitated. There were final answers here, answers that concerned Maria alone. And then all at once, she nodded. She would not desert her friend. Not now. "Come on," she said. "We'll go together and see what the waters have left behind."

Slowly they climbed down the muddy slopes to the dripping floor of Lake Ere towards the white curving shapes which lay revealed there.

Like a hand beckoning, it drew them onwards. But its message was for Maria, not Philippa.

As they picked their way over the damp and dripping land left by the lake, Maria kept her eyes fastened on the bones of white stretching towards her.

Not bones. They stopped, slightly breathless, and Maria shaded her eyes against the sun. A filigree design of white marble, an ornate pavilion, rising from the slippery, bedraggled valley floor. It was draped round with weed and silt, and yet gold leaf shone from its roof, sparkled in the water-cleansed sunlight.

It was somewhere very special, somewhere specially honoured. Maria frowned. She had seen architecture like that only once before, decorating the tomb of her maternal grandmother. In the Gardens of Remembrance at Soprafini, an elegant fantasy of a sepulchre rose high above the other graves and tombs, set with precious stones and gems, as this was.

"It's a tomb," said Philippa, shivering. Suddenly she knew she could go no further. This was a place of grief and pain, and it was nothing to do with her. She had been the watchman, that was all. The herald, the messenger. This was not her story. "I'll wait here, if you don't mind. . . ."

Maria pressed her hand and turned away.

She walked slowly across the muddy pebbles, over the green drenched weed and sky-coloured pools.

A hundred metres away Maria could see that a small sarcophagus lay at the centre of the pavilion.

She drew nearer.

The coffin was tiny, that of a small baby. It was made of the finest marble, and there was lettering on its upper surface.

She cleared the silt from the engraved script with hands which trembled strangely.

> *Here lies the beloved and only daughter*
> *of Gregor and Olivia of Soprafini.*
> *Cruelly cursed, our little darling.*
> *Maria Soprafini, Crown Princess.*

Her own name. She, herself, buried there as a child. . . .

At first she was too shocked, too confused to take in the sense of it. Some other Gregor and Olivia . . . But to her certain knowledge, there were no others, not in the entire history of Soprafini. Only her parents, only the people she had called Father and Mother.

She was their only child, she had no sister, there had been no other lost baby girl. . . .

There were dates below the inscription. With hands that were now almost helpless with fear, she cleared the muck away.

Her own birthday was engraved there. And the death date, only six months later.

Who was this? What had happened?

Was *this* why the valley had been drowned?

And like a sledgehammer, the answers fell into place. She knew exactly and completely what had happened. The inscription told everything, gave it all away.

Gregor and Olivia had had one child, one little darling daughter, Maria. That child had died, cursed, so the inscription said. But the treaties had been signed, the marriage arranged long ago and they did not want to back down. Knowing the Rustrians, they could not afford to.

And so another child had grown up in the

princess's place, an orphan child perhaps, trained and groomed to fulfil the role. No expense had been spared, no honour and dignity denied. No one had known that she was not the real princess.

Maria was stunned with shock. She stood rooted to that muddy place while her mind raced around her life, her parents, how it had all seemed. . . .

And the truth of it lay in something that no one could measure or prove. She knew it in her bones, that was all. Gregor and Olivia did not love her. They had always been cold and distantly formal to her, and she had known nothing else, had seen it as natural for kings and queens never to laugh with their children, never to hug or kiss them. They had done their duty, but there had never been any affection there, not the least gesture of warmth or kindliness.

She was not their daughter: why should they waste emotion on a stranger?

Her whole lifetime had been a cheat.

Maria, not of Soprafini, not of anywhere at all that she knew, felt very unsteady. Her knees gave way.

She knelt in the mud, her head in her hands, and wept.

The lonely child, her ghostly namesake, the

cursed, unremembered stranger at the Court of Soprafini, wept with her.

They had both been cheated of childhood and love.

Gregor viewed the bedraggled remnants of the Rustrian army with an emotion more powerful than satisfaction. It was relief, strong and over-whelming. He had just received command of the army from one of the few surviving Rustrian generals.

Ferrian's body had been discovered an hour earlier, clinging round the back of a dark-haired man who had only one hand. They seemed to have dragged each other down . . . All the Rustrian artillery, all their Fireflies and pyro-mancers had been lost.

For the first time Gregor of Soprafini, his own small, highly-trained army on top form, found that he could make his own terms.

He was busy drawing up the agreement, and only part of his mind worried about what was revealed on the valley floor.

But Olivia remembered. She was gripped by a desire to see once more the last resting place of her only child. She called her most trusted serving maid and ordered their litter to be carried down to the valley floor.

The journey took some time, for the going

was treacherous with mud and silt, and difficult for the litter-bearers to negotiate. But eventually Olivia ordered them to stop. She left her litter and sent the men away. Supported by her maid-servants, she picked her away over the muddy flats to the tomb of her daughter.

Maria stood up unsteadily, her face like ash.

The woman she'd known as mother looked at her coolly.

"Well, I suppose it worked in the end," Olivia said slowly. "The Rustrian threat is over, although not how we'd planned. . . ."

"Mother—?" What else could Maria call her? "What shall I do now?"

The queen was too elegant to shrug. She raised her eyebrows. "There is no need for pretence any more. As you now know, I am not your mother. You will not suffer, of course . . . It seems you have served us well, after all. A life-time's pension, a house somewhere, servants, whatever you want—"

"If you are not my mother, who *am* I?" Maria hardly took in what Olivia was saying.

"No one in particular. A serving maid's bastard, that's all. She died, I think . . . there are details somewhere if you're interested. But no royal blood runs in your veins, girl, although your fingers are at least straight and perfectly formed."

"What do you mean?"

"She was deformed. My only daughter, deformed. Cursed at birth with webbed fingers—"

"Webbed? Was she *arethusan*?"

"It happens sometimes, the doctors said. A throwback, a freak. . . ."

"What happened to her?"

"She – could not live—"

"Did you *kill* her?" Horror in Maria's voice. She backed away from the woman she had once called mother.

Olivia's lips were tight. "She died. That is all you need to know."

It was too much to comprehend.

"What are you going to do?" Olivia's voice was cold.

"What *can* I do? Where shall I go? Can't I come home?"

"It's not your home." The woman moved forward, and put a hand on the tomb of her only child. Her eyes were bright with tears. *Beloved*, it read. *Little darling.* "I don't really want to see you again."

Maria took half a step towards her and then stopped.

Tears, falling again.

"At last, at last, I can mourn my daughter," said the queen.

Maria turned away from her. There were muddy wastes all around her, broken trees and dead wood, all the debris of the draining flood. She saw a fish flapping helplessly as one of the muddy pools dried in the autumn sun. She bent down, holding it in her two hands.

Unsteadily she walked to the deep flowing river that now ran through the valley. She let the fish go and watched its tail glimmer once in the sun.

When she turned round, Josquin was there, his blond hair tied back in a velvet ribbon, his slight figure graceful in Soprafinian clothes. She did not hesitate, but went straight to him.

His arms folded around her. "Come with me," he said. "I'll take you home."

"Home? But I don't know where that is!" she cried. "I have no home, no name, nothing—"

"Ssssh, all it means is that you're free. You can be who you want, what you want . . ." He touched her cheek, smiling gently. "And anyway, what's in a name? They're two a penny . . . You're the Lady of Song, the Princess of the High C, the leading star in Miracule's firmament . . ." He was laughing, but his eyes were quite serious. "There's a family waiting for you, although they're a bit eccentric. Could you bear a mermaid for a mother-in-law?"

"What?" She didn't understand.

"The Lady Aqurelt," he whispered. "Don't tell anyone. She's a mermaid, after all. It's true. In water she swims like any fish, like our little Philippa friend. She's Philippa's mother . . . She made the same choice as Philippa has. To live on land for the sake of love . . . Reckless, all of them. The Lady's an arethusan, a true mermaid. She's my dear and adopted mother. Mother to us all."

Maria laughed softly. "And so Philippa knows who she is, what she is . . . An arethusan! To think I never saw it. There was so much I never saw . . ." She leant her head on his shoulder. He felt warm and dry and comfortable. And then he took her by the hand and pulled her up the slippery, muddy slope towards Philippa, and she didn't even look back to the woman kneeling in the mud by a tomb.

The tomb of the real Princess Maria of Soprafini, who had had webbed hands.

Maria was free.

They found Gerain waiting at the top of the slope. He looked hot and uncomfortable in the formal Soprafinian wear they had all been given.

"I've had enough of this place. Look at this!" He flicked one of his lacy cuffs in disgust. "All dressed up like a dog's dinner and nowhere to go. Let's get out of here, shall we?" he said.

"Do you mean to Barusi?" asked Philippa.

"No . . . There's nothing there for me. Not now that Marco's dead and the arethusans are free . . . I don't want to go back there." He looked at Josquin. "I want to go home. To Miracule and the Lady. Teach me to juggle, Jos? I think I'd like to try the burning clubs, or how about knives—?"

Philippa grinned at him and stood on tiptoe to kiss his cheek.

Josquin took him by the arm. "It's all a question of rhythm," he said. "And practice, of course. What you do, is. . . ."

Maria and Philippa set off after them.

They would be travelling together.

Look out for the next title in the Point Fantasy *series:*

The Emperor Mage
Tamora Pierce

Silver light filled the cabin; a heavy, musky smell drifted in the air. When the light, if not the smell, faded, a badger sat on the bunk where Kitten slept. —*Begone, pest,*— he ordered.

The rat was brave in the way of his kind, but the smell of *this* friend of Daine's sent the rodent into his hole. He had not known Daine was on visiting terms with the badger god.

Daine smiled at the first owner of her silver claw. "You look well. How long's it been?"

The badger was not in the least interested in polite conversation. —*Why are you here?*— he demanded harshly. —*What possessed you to leave your home sett? You are a creature of pine and chestnut forests, and cold lakes. This hot, swampy land is no country for you! Why are you here?*—

Daine made a face. "I'll tell you, if you'll stop growling at me." She sat on the bunk opposite him, and explained what the Tortallans in general, and she in particular, were doing this far south.

The badger listened, growling softly to himself. —*Peace? I thought your humans were convinced Emperor Ozorne was the one who tore holes in the barriers between the human realms and the realms of the gods, to loose a plague of immortals on you.—*

Daine shrugged. "*He* says it wasn't him or his mages who did that. Renegades at the imperial university stole the unlocking spells. They were caught and tried last spring, and executed." The badger snorted. "Well, no one can prove if it's the truth or not. And the king says we need peace with Carthak more than we need to get revenge."

—No one needs to talk peace or any other thing here. This is the worst possible place you can be now. You have no idea . . . Turn around and go home. Convince your friends to leave.—

"I can't, and *we* can't!" she protested. "Weren't you listening? The emperor knows I'm coming to look at his birds. If I go home now, when he expects me – think of the insult to him! And it's not the birds' fault they live here, is it?"

With no room for him to pace, he was forced to settle for shifting his bulk from one side to the other as he muttered to himself. *—I must talk them out of it, that's all. When they know – even they will have to understand the situation. It's not like a mortal girl has the freedom they do, after all.—*

"Who will understand?" Daine asked, intensely curious. In all the time she had known him, she had never seen him so uncertain, or so jittery. Like all badgers, he had rages, and would knock her top over tea-kettle if she vexed him, but that was very different from the way he acted now. "And what's going on here? Can't you tell me?"

—*It's the greater gods, the ones two-leggers worship,*— the badger replied. —*They have lost patience with the emperor, perhaps with this entire realm. Things could get very – chancy – here soon. You are sure you cannot make your friends turn back?*—

Daine shook her head.

—*No, of course not. You said it was impossible, and you never mislead me.*— Suddenly he cocked his head upward, as if listening to something, or someone. He growled, hackles rising, and snapped at the air. Then – slowly – he relaxed, and nodded. —*As you wish.*—

"As who wishes?" asked Daine.

He looked at her, an odd light in his eyes. —*Come here, Daine.*—

"What?" she asked, even as she obeyed.

—*I have a gift for you. Something to help you if all goes ill.*—

He had given her lessons before, in the use of her wild magic, but not gifts, and his words had made her edgy. "Badger, I can't misbehave while I'm here. There's too much at stake. You ought to talk to Duke Gareth of Naxen. You know every time you teach me a lesson or give me a gift or anything, there's always an uncommon lot of ruction, and I've been told not to cause *any*!"

—Enough! Kneel!—

She had thought to refuse, but her knees bent, and she was face to face with him. Opening his jaws, the great animal breathed on her. His breath came out visible, a swirling fog that glowed bright silver. It wrapped around Daine's head, filling her nose, mouth and eyes, trickling under her shirt, flowing down her arms. She gasped, and the mist ran deep into her throat and lungs. She could feel it throughout her body, expanding to fill her skin.

When her eyes cleared, he was gone.

POINT SF

Encounter worlds where men and women make
hazardous voyages through space; where time travel is a
reality and the fifth dimension a possibility; where the
ultimate horror has already happened and mankind
breaks through the barrier of technology . . .

The Obernewtyn Chronicles:
Book 1: Obernewtyn
Book 2: The Farseekers
Isobelle Carmody
A new breed of humans are born into a hostile world
struggling back from the brink of apocalypse . . .

Random Factor
Jessica Palmer
Battle rages in space. War has been erased from earth and is
now controlled by an all-powerful computer – until a random
factor enters the system . . .

First Contact
Nigel Robinson
In 1992 mankind launched the search for extra-terrestial
intelligence. Two hundred years later, someone responded . . .

Virus
Molly Brown
A mysterious virus is attacking the staff of an engineering plant
. . . Who, or *what* is responsible?

Look out for:

Strange Orbit
Margaret Simpson

Scatterlings
Isobelle Carmody

Body Snatchers
Stan Nicholls

Read Point SF and enter a new dimension . . .